CF Sa31a

Salassi, Otto R.

And nobody knew they were
there

AND NOBODY KNEW
THEY WERE THERE

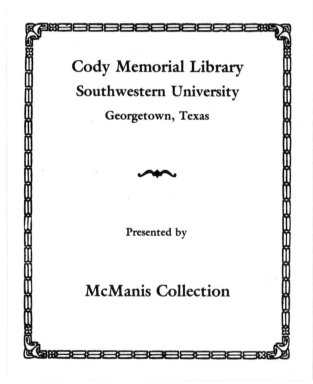

OTTO R. SALASSI

And Nobody Knew They Were There

 GREENWILLOW BOOKS
NEW YORK

Library of Congress Cataloging in Publication Data
Salassi, Otto R.
And nobody knew they were there.
Summary: For reasons of its own, a squad of
Marines disappears after a recruiting assignment
at a Houston fairgrounds; but its discovery by two
thirteen-year-old boys jeopardizes its plans.
[1. Adventure and adventurers—Fiction]
I. Title.   PZ7.S1478An 1984   [Fic]   83-16487
ISBN 0-688-00940-9

TO MAX AND ADAM

CONTENTS

Part Two: The Partisans 55

Part Three: The Bridge 139

Epilogue 171

**AND NOBODY KNEW
THEY WERE THERE**

PREFACE

The Disappearance

Houston, Texas,
June 8, 1956

It was the kind of night they'd hoped for, with no moon and no wind, and Sims slowed the jeep to a crawling stop. He was on his way back to the squad with extra batteries, which they might or might not need but which he'd gone after just the same. What he'd really wanted was a chance to think everything over one last time, and his best thinking was always done alone.

In front of the jeep arching the road was the gateway to the Harris County Fairgrounds, and a yellow banner stretched under the arch told visitors that it was "Armed Forces Week, June 4–9." A billboard off to the side of the road listed the main events that had been scheduled for the week. The Air Force had

3

trucked in the fuselage of a B-29 and was letting people crawl around in it. The Coast Guard had been launching balloons every hour and putting on demonstrations of how weather is predicted. Friday had been a big day with an Army unit from Fort Hood in Killeen putting on a tank show. Tomorrow was supposed to be the biggest day of all, with the Navy's Blue Angels and the Air Force's Thunderbirds both scheduled to fly in and with a 1,000-man parachute drop from the 101st Airborne planned in commemoration of the anniversary of the week of D-Day.

And what had the Fighting Marines come up with to match that kind of glamour? Tomorrow was their biggest day, and on their biggest day Groh and Lofton were scheduled to put on a bayonet drill, Jenkins and Three-Finger Hopper were supposed to show off in hand-to-hand combat, and Peterson was scheduled, every half hour on the half hour, to crank up his flamethrower and scorch some gophers. The big difference was that Peterson wasn't going to be there in the morning, because the squad wasn't going to be there in the morning, because they were all going to be somewhere else.

Near the billboard was another sign, a smaller one that was barely visible in the jeep's headlights, one with an outline of a thermometer painted on it. Armed Forces Week just happened to coincide with high school graduations in that area of Texas, and recruiters had hoped to sign up as many as 500 new volunteers. The "temperature" on the sign was red to the 480 mark, and all the outfits except the Marines had reached their quotas. The Marines had hoped to get 100; but at last count they'd gotten only 13, and half of the 13 looked as if they couldn't pass the physical.

Since Tuesday Sims and the eight men of his squad had been living in the field behind the cattle barns, where they'd set up a typical artillery OP, which signs explained was short for observation post. They had dug in, fortified the OP with sandbags, and set up machine guns the way they'd have done in World War II or Korea if they'd had the time. They had a galley and a latrine; the whole idea—and it was the lieutenant's idea, not Sims's—was to live in it, eat, sleep, and stink in it, and it would look so real that kids would want to join up.

Dumb. And if living in a hole in the ground and pretending you were in some John Wayne movie weren't enough to show people how dumb you were, tomorrow—the dumbest of the lieutenant's dumb ideas—Peterson was going to turn on that stinking flamethrower and burn some stinking gophers.

Except Peterson wasn't going to be there in the morning.

Sims put the jeep back in gear and drove on under the arch and through the empty fairgrounds, on toward the exhibit and cattle barns near the back. Four of the barns were lit up, but the fifth one in the row, the one assigned to the marines, was dark. There was a big party going on in the first barn, and as Sims got closer, he could hear singing. The song was an old ballad that had been kicked around barracks and boot camps forever:

> Oh, dear, what can the matter be?
> Seven old ladies trapped in a lavatory.
> They were there from Monday to Saturday,
> And nobody knew they were there.

He slowed the jeep for a moment and looked in. All the recruiting outfits were there with two GI cans iced down and loaded with beer. The Navy had a crap game going, and it was the Air Force doing the terrible howling.

> The first to go in was old Mrs. Humphrey.
> She just went in to make herself comfy.
> But when she sat down, she couldn't get her
>   rump free,
> And nobody knew she was there.

The only marine at the party was the lieutenant, shirt off, down on his hands and knees, pleading with the dice to be nice. The other marine recruiters lived in Houston and would be home with their wives and kiddies. The men in his squad would be waiting in the hole.

He parked the jeep with the others in the makeshift motor pool at the end of the row of barns and got out.

The men in his squad were a special bunch of marines. Jones, who'd be their guide, could read a topo map and see everything, just like he was looking at a picture. Three-Finger Billy Hopper was the squad's rigger. He'd cut off two of the fingers on his right hand on a high school power saw, but he could do more with a coil of rope or a spool of crossing cable than any man alive. Jenkins used to burgle houses in the San Diego area. Even after he had joined the Marines and been to Korea, he slipped off base every once in a while and burgled some houses. No one had ever caught him at it, but everyone suspected him of doing it. Groh had been a medic in Korea and was in charge of blisters and pain. Russell could cook and generally knew what was edible and not. Lofton could swim and do other tricks. Once he'd won a bet by staying underwater and holding his breath longer than a diving duck; the duck had come up gasping. Peterson wasn't too smart, but he could carry a ton. Ross couldn't do anything, or rather, he could do everything, but nothing very well. His special talent was that he thought of things. He thought of things nobody else could think of.

Like Sims, all the men of the squad were wearing combat fatigues, green with brown, black, and splotches for camouflage. They wore the same kind of camouflage cap, pulled down low over their foreheads with just enough room to see out. In the dark, if Sims hadn't known them so well, he wouldn't have been able to tell them apart. Except for Peterson, they were so much alike in size that they could easily wear each other's clothes, and before this trip was over, they probably would.

When Sims started climbing into the harness of his backpack, they started getting into theirs. They had twenty-six days to cover 450 miles; and that meant averaging 15 miles a day, but if their plans were good they'd make it. On their way to Houston they had hidden everything they'd need: food, maps, and extra equipment. They had set up the supply caches to divide the trip into thirds: ten days to the first one near Jasper, Texas, ten days to the next one in an old barn in Louisiana, six days if they needed them to get to the last one, the one with the ropes and stuff they'd need at the end. Things were so well planned there was no reason to hope for good luck; the only thing Sims hoped for was no bad luck.

"If something happens and we don't make it, it's the brig for me and bad times for the rest of you. They'll probably send you to the Rock." The Rock was Okinawa, and a sane person would rather shoot off his foot than get sent there. They'd been through this before, but Sims felt he had to give them one more chance to think about it.

"But if we make it, we'll be heroes," Jenkins pointed out. It never entered his mind that there was some job he couldn't pull off, and the reason he'd joined the Marines was to get a chance to be a hero.

"If we make it, they'll talk about us for years."

That was Groh. He liked the idea of being a legend in his own time, and even in the dark you could tell he was crazy. The reason he wasn't a medic anymore was that he was crazy and you didn't feel quite safe with him giving you shots.

The drunken choir in the barn had finally come to the last verse in the song:

> The last to go in was old Mrs. Myrtle.
> She just went in to tighten her girdle.
> But she didn't have a dime, so she tried a high hurdle,
> And nobody knew she was there.

They listened to the singing without saying anything; nobody had anything that needed saying.

"Then let's do it," Sims said, and their trip began. They darkened their faces and hands with shoe polish and one by one crawled out of their hole. Running in a low crouch, they crossed the field behind the barns to the line of trees and the dry creek bed that was there. The creek bed would take them north and east into open country.

A single paragraph in the "News in Brief" section of the Houston afternoon newspaper the next day would read:

SEND IN THE MARINES?
A Marine recruiting officer reported to Houston police that nine men disappeared during the night and are

listed as AWOL. The men are part of a special demonstration unit assigned to recruiting duty and have
been taking part in the recruiting drive that ended to-
day at the fairgrounds. Anyone seeing the missing
men are asked to contact the Houston police department.

A whole squad of nine marines did not disappear
that often, and one week later, when they were still
missing, the men would be identified by name and
their pictures would be printed in the newspapers and
appear on television. In ten days people everywhere
would start seeing them. A farmer in Arkansas would
call the sheriff and report that he'd seen nine marines
stealing his chickens and had chased them away with
his gun. A woman with psychic abilities in New
Jersey would call the police and tell them about a
dream she had in which she saw nine Americans in a
prison cell in some strange country that she thought
was Russia. A high school science teacher in Ohio
would go on television to say how he had evidence
that the marines were on board a UFO but that the
military authorities were ignoring him.

This story begins twenty days after the first news
article appeared in the Houston paper, in a little town
most people never heard of.

PART ONE

The Discovery

1: The Strain of
Human Kindness

There isn't much worth remembering about the year 1956. Unless it happened to be the year somebody was born, graduated from school, got married, made a million dollars, or had some other reason to remember it, people tend to forget it altogether. To the two boys in this story, Hogan McGhee and his cousin from Memphis, Jakey Darby, 1956 would be the best year of their lives, or one of the best. The morning before it all started for them, though, it didn't seem that way.

Hogan McGhee was suffering under the strain of human kindness. An hour before the train was due from Shreveport, he was still getting fussed at—

"talked to" might be a better way of putting it, since his father never really fussed at anybody.

"Kids growing up in the city don't have the same advantages kids in the country do," his father was saying. All Hogan had done was mention at breakfast that he hoped his cousin Jakey hated it there on the farm and wanted to go back to Memphis, and right away he knew he'd said the wrong thing. First he got a lecture on how his cousin Jakey didn't have a father anymore and how Jakey's mother, a woman alone in the world, needed some help.

That led to the subject of basic human kindness and how it was everybody's God-given duty to be kind to those less fortunate than themselves. Hogan's father was famous for his lectures. All over the parish they talked about what a fine man he was and how they'd drive anywhere in Louisiana to hear him preach a sermon and how it was a shame that he wasn't a real preacher. The truth of the matter was that Hogan, his three sisters, his mother, and grandmother would drive anywhere in the *world* to get out of listening.

All breakfast long, his three sisters were loving it. There was nothing they liked better than seeing him get lectured to.

After breakfast, after they'd loaded into the bus and were on their way to the station to pick up poor cousin Jakey, he was still getting fussed at, talked to, lectured to, preached to, or whatever anybody wanted to call it.

"... and you and he are going to have to get along without fighting ..."

That was coming from his father.

"... and you're just going to have to make up your mind to do some of the things *he* wants to do ..."

That was from his mother.

"... and when you go places, he goes with you. Don't leave him sitting at home with nothing to do. ..."

That was from his father again, and that's the way it went, all the way to the train station in Natchitoches, the big old church bus creaking and groaning, his father and mother grinding out instruction after instruction, his sisters loving it.

He didn't mind not fighting, since fighting wasn't something he did for fun anyway. And he could live with the idea of doing some of the things his cousin wanted to do, so long as they didn't interfere with his own plans. But as for the instructions to take Jakey everywhere he went, he'd rather be lying on the stone-hard floor of hell with his back broken than carry a dumb city-boy cousin around with him all summer.

Wisely, however, he kept his mouth shut. His friends at school called him Crazy McGhee sometimes because sometimes he did crazy things. Nobody ever called him Stupid McGhee, though, unless he was looking for trouble.

And there were ways to handle a city boy in the country. There was poison ivy, snakes, skunks, and lots of other things that were even better: getting him lost in the woods, leaving him stranded in the brake and making him wade back. There were some mean things he could do, like getting him to say something dumb to his sisters about their big ears.

They could hear the train a long time before they could see it, and the pigs in the stockcar on the loading track could hear it, too, and were nervous. It was like they knew they were about to take a train ride that they didn't want to take.

"He's been in trouble with the police; since his father died, he's had a chip on his shoulder; he didn't want to come here, so he's liable to be tough and defensive. . . ." They were outside on the platform, everybody except Grandma McGhee, who had a hard time getting up and down the church bus steps. His father was giving them all last-minute instructions, this time talking to the girls as well as to him. "I want you all to remember that and give him a lot of room." He had a lot more to say; but the train was there, and he couldn't talk over the noise.

And then the train stopped. The conductor came out and put down the metal step for the passengers who were getting off or in this case the passenger, since there was only one. Deep in Hogan's heart he'd been wishing that something would happen and his cousin wouldn't show up, but that wasn't the case. The boy who got off the train was wearing blue jeans, a pink shirt, white shoes, and his hair was long and greasy, like a Memphis punk. The first thing he did was put down his suitcase, take out his comb, and start combing his hair in what was clearly a duck's butt.

He was the same age and the same weight as Hogan—their birthdays weren't a month apart—but he was heavier, like he never played sports or anything. He walked across the platform toward them, wrinkling his nose like he was doing them a big favor by coming to visit them, instead of their doing him one by letting him come. Hogan walked forward with the rest of the family to meet him halfway.

When they met, before Hogan's mother could throw her arms around her nephew, before anybody could do anything, Jakey stopped and swung the suitcase and his back around till he was looking the other way, threw his nose up in the air, and starting sniffing like a black dog on the prowl. When he turned back around, nobody, Hogan included, was sure what to say, and his cousin got in the first words.

And the first words weren't anything simple, like "Hello, I'm Jakey Darby," or "Hello, are you the McGhees?" Hogan's Memphis city-boy cousin's first words were "What stinks?" That was it: "What stinks?"

2: A Sure Sign of Trouble

What stunk to Jakey's unfamiliar nose was nothing more than the pigs in the stockcar on the sidetrack, waiting in the sun to go to market. Pigs do not smell good, as a rule, but Hogan didn't know of anything that could be done about it. There wasn't anything you could do about it, except pretend you couldn't smell them, which is what most people did.

It surprised Hogan somewhat, his cousin's walking up and acting like he did, and in that first performance Hogan's opinion of him was changed. His cousin wasn't going to be a drag who didn't know anything; his cousin was smart, sure of himself, and maybe even dangerous. He thought about it and decided to be careful in what he planned. When you were dealing with somebody smart, your plans might backfire.

They said their hellos then, and everybody got introduced, except Grandma McGhee, who was waiting in the bus. They started walking out to the bus for that very purpose, figuring she'd be mad if they kept her waiting too long. And when Jakey saw the bus for the first time, he did something again that was the complete opposite of what was expected, and made Hogan again revise his opinion.

The bus wasn't anything but a regular old church bus, exactly like a school bus, of which there had to be millions, except instead of being painted yellow, it was painted purple and gold. Now purple and gold are supposed to have some kind of religious meaning, Hogan knew, but those two colors just didn't go together, and there was nothing you could do to make them. The bus was painted purple on top and gold on the bottom, and it was ugly, just plain ugly.

So what does Jakey Darby do? He throws both hands up in the air and yells, "Wow, what a beaut!" He runs out ahead of everybody else and starts making a big to-do over it, looking at the front and the back and feeling the paint like he wanted to make sure it was real. "St. Maurice Church"; he reads the name from the side. By that time Hogan and his family weren't just surprised; they were more like flabbergasted. Nobody liked that bus but his father, who was beaming with pride.

Hogan revised his opinion to emphasize the *smart* part. Jakey Darby was going to be very smart.

By the time they got to the bus, even before they got there, they could hear Grandma McGhee fussing, asking what was taking so long, and complaining about how you weren't supposed to leave a dog inside a hot bus, much less an old lady. When Jakey got on the bus, she grabbed him up in her meaty old arms and almost smothered him.

"Take it easy, Grandma." Jakey laughed and told her, "You gonna get all excited and start croaking on us."

In Hogan's mind that was near blasphemy, but Jakey got away with it. Grandma McGhee started laughing and talking like she seldom ever did. "Croaking," she said. "People been expecting me to start croaking since I was fifty."

Trouble, Hogan was thinking, a pure and simple sign of trouble.

3: Jakey's Best Behavior

The train ride from Memphis had been long and boring, but it had given Jakey plenty of time to think and work out a good strategy. His mother had given him his own set of specialized instructions, and they were a lot tougher than Hogan's. Not only did they include not fighting and the same kinds of things Hogan got, but they included some even harder orders as well, orders that were not just hard, but impossible to follow. He was told to be on his best behavior, which he might be able to be for a little while, if he absolutely had to, but certainly not for a whole summer. He wasn't sure, though, what his best behavior was. He did things that were wrong sometimes, like saying what he thought out loud and saying funny things, but there were other times when doing the exact same thing was considered the right thing to do. His mother's orders to be careful didn't make sense because saying the wrong thing came just as naturally as saying the right thing. There wasn't anything to be careful about.

His strategy was simply to try to say the right thing and let his country cousins like it or lump it. He got off the train and saw them standing there, with haircuts so short they looked too dumb to count money, and he thought of what he possibly might say. Luckily there was that smell in the air waiting for him. Natchitoches, Louisiana, stank, like a cat's graveyard, and he'd said so.

When he saw the bus, he might have said how funny-looking it was, sitting there in the middle of an empty parking lot, painted like it was, with the door open and his fat grandma sitting in the front seat, talking to herself ninety miles an hour, looking like it wanted to take them all not just to the St. Maurice Church but to that great reward in the sky. He might have said something funny, but that would've been wrong, so all he did was praise it. He was going to try to praise everything.

When he got in trouble with the police, even though it hadn't been his fault—he'd simply been in the wrong place at the wrong time—his mother'd come down on him, watching his every move, not letting him do anything with his friends, always bugging him about his homework. So he'd decided to run away to Texas. He'd saved enough money to take the bus to Little Rock, but when the bus pulled in, the police were waiting for him and put him on another one back to Memphis again.

That was when she decided to send him to Louisiana, and if he did well, she'd loosen up on him. That was the bargain.

She'd even send him five dollars a week so he could go to all the movies. Going to the movies was the single best thing he liked to do, and when he grew up, he was going to be in the movies himself. And why not? He was going to be tall, and he wasn't bad-looking. He knew he knew a lot more about movies than anybody his age, and he knew what he had to do to get to act in them.

The first thing to be was from someplace like Texas and not someplace like Memphis. When he was a star and they talked about him, they'd say how he ran away from home after his father died and became a cowboy.

But that would all have to wait till he was older. Thirteen was too young to be a cowboy in Texas he'd found out; something else was just going to have to do for a while.

The McGhees didn't take Jakey straight home; that would have been too simple. Grandma McGhee wanted to take her grandson around and show him the town, so they drove around in the bus for a while and saw the sights. A visit from a grandson was an important occasion for Grandma McGhee, and she didn't get out of the house for many occasions.

Jakey got to see the historic downtown: the oldest permanent settlement in the Louisiana Purchase, Fort Seldon, where American troops got ready to invade Mexico; a bunch of old houses that were still there because people still lived in them; and finally, a place called Grand Écore, which was a big outdoor theater on the bluff above the Red River, where they put on musicals from New York like *My Fair Lady* and *Oklahoma!* Jakey wouldn't mind being in a play if he could get the right part. After Grand Écore, Grandma McGhee got tired, and they headed home. "Think you'll like it here?" Aunt Lucy asked him, and he was sorely tempted to say no.

"Don't seem like a whole lot to do," he ended up answering. He'd only seen one walk-in and one drive-in theater. The show at the walk-in was *Bad Day at Black Rock,* which had already been out a year in Memphis and everybody had seen it.

"I thought I might take him camping," Hogan offered, like it was out of the kindness of his heart, "or maybe fishing over in Alligator Slough."

Hogan was sitting behind all the others, about half-way down the long bus, and he couldn't see anything but the back of his father's head and his eyes in the rearview mirror. The trouble was he didn't have to see any more to know his father was frowning.

"No," his father said, "I've got another plan in mind."

4: The Duel

Hogan never thought about the farm's being a long way from town before, but on the ride back that first morning with his newly arrived cousin, that's what he began to think. If the farm were closer, walking distance or even bicycling distance, he and Jakey wouldn't be so glued together. He didn't feel a kinship to Jakey, had never thought very much about him, and did not, in fact, even know very much about him. Hogan's father, Gilbert McGhee, had a younger sister named Shirley, after Shirley Temple. Aunt Shirley had married a man named George Darby, who was stationed at Camp Polk during the war, and after the war they'd moved to Memphis. They had one kid, Jakey, who was born one month and three days later than Hogan, making Hogan one month and three days older. George Darby had died of a heart attack two years ago, and instead of coming home, as everybody thought she'd do, Shirley had gone to work as a legal secretary. That was all Hogan knew about the Darbys, except for the trouble that Jakey had been in. Jakey had been in some kind of gang fight in a big city park and picked up by the police. Aunt Shirley had had to go to the police station with the lawyer she worked for to get him out of jail. Then two months ago Jakey had tried to run away from home, and the police had caught him again. That was why he'd come to live with them, to get out of Memphis, to stay out of trouble for a while.

Like Hogan, Jakey rode the bus in silence, dreading every mile that the bus was putting between him and civilization. Unlike Hogan, though, who was merely staring out the window, Jakey was actually looking at things and trying to memorize everything: turns, directions, road numbers, and landmarks. He wanted to be able to get away if he had to, and knowing the way back to town could be important.

They'd crossed the Red River and headed east on U.S. 84 for about eleven miles. They crossed the Saline Bayou and the Natches Bayou, and right after the Natches, they'd turned due south onto a gravel road and gone about four miles, then slowed down and stopped on a narrow dirt farm road beside an old church.

"That's our church," his uncle Gilbert told him. "McGhees as far back as the 1820's are buried in there."

"In there" was an ancient graveyard covered with weeds.

The dirt farm road led west, back toward the river and Natchitoches. At first Jakey thought the bus was too wide for the road; it bounced around on its springs like at any moment it might decide to bounce off in a ditch. Limbs and bushes scraped against the sides and made loud scratching noises. The dust behind the bus was so thick the back seats got darker from the lack of sunlight.

"All this is the farm," his aunt told him. So far he and Hogan hadn't said a word to each other.

The farm wasn't 100 percent gloomy, but it was a good 50. There were open fields with some kind of green vegetable matter growing in them, and there was another field which was full of cows eating the vegetable matter. Here and there, between the fields and alongside the road, were big, slimy-looking green bogs so overgrown with trees and bushes that it looked like the sun never got through. When they got to the house, it looked like something out of an old movie with big-limbed "hanging trees" everywhere with moss all over them. Dueling trees, he decided, and he could imagine somebody like Errol Flynn or Clark Gable with pistols in his hands under any one of them.

When they got off the bus, not an easy thing to do with Grandma McGhee needing help to get down the stairs and insisting on Hogan and Jakey's helping her down and then not letting them go till she'd given them each a big kiss, Jakey took a long look at the house. It was two-story and white and was old and needed painting. It had a long, wide porch with a roof over it, running across the whole front of the house, and the windows were the tall kind that stayed open like doors and you could walk through them. It wasn't exactly a mansion because it wasn't big enough or fancy enough, and it didn't have columns all across the front; but it was a lot better than his own house in Memphis, and there was a brass plaque mounted on the wall by the door naming the house, "McGhee House," giving the date it was built, "1859," and declaring it an official historic house.

The house and the trees were the best things Jakey had seen since leaving Memphis, but instead of making him feel good, they made him feel worse. He felt he didn't belong there, and it was a strange feeling. He felt he didn't belong anywhere, and when he realized that everybody was waiting for him to say something, he felt like saying the wrong thing on purpose.

"I'm surprised you don't have bars on all the windows," he heard himself saying. "Don't you think I might get away?"

Instead of being surprised by his cousin's strange manner this time, Hogan could understand it. He felt two things at once: his cousin's anger and the chip on his shoulder. When he looked up at his father, his father gave him a nod, and his eyes weren't frowning. "I'll take the suitcase in," his father said. "Why don't you show Jakey around the farm?"

5: A Flip of the Coin

Gilbert and Lucy McGhee stood watching from the front room window as their son and their nephew walked off together to tour the farm. The girls had wanted to go, too, but Gilbert McGhee said no. "The boys need time together," he said. "And I want them to get it." He hoped they would be friends, and if that happened, he had a better reason to hope that Shirley would move back home for good. He and his sister had talked about it over the phone.

Two boys growing up together on a farm in Louisiana . . . summertime . . . fishing . . . hunting together . . . just sitting on the porch and whittling on a stick. . . . There wasn't a better life anywhere in the world.

He smiled to see Butterbean, Hogan's fat old beagle, stir herself awake, stretch, and waddle off after them. Butterbean usually stirred only to eat or to get one of the girls to scratch her outrageous belly.

The farm was arranged so that the corners of all four fields met on an access road that swung around the house from north of it to south. The family called the fields by their compass directions from the house—south, southeast, northeast, and north—and called them fields instead of pastures because the

McGhees still considered themselves farmers, not ranchers.

"We run what's called a feeder farm," Hogan was saying. The two boys were on the access road, walking slowly toward the north field, and Hogan was making an effort at explaining how the farm worked. It wasn't much of an effort, though, and mostly the two were feeling each other out. "We plant sweet sorghum for silage and corn and grain; we keep two fields in clover."

"Sounds exciting," Jakey said. He didn't know what silage was and didn't want to know. The same was true of sorghum.

"My father buys two hundred yearlings from the auction every six months or so. We fatten them up on the clover, silage, and grain and sell them," Hogan went on, trying to be serious in what was clearly an impossible situation.

They stood at the gate to the north field and looked at 200 yearling calves sitting on their bellies in the hot sun, chewing their cuds. "Yummy, yummy," Jakey said, turning his back to the field and leaning on the gate behind him with his elbows on the top rail.

Hogan didn't pride himself on knowing much about human nature. He had always trusted his instincts, and sometimes his instincts had been wrong. In this case, though, he felt that he couldn't be wrong.

Cousin Jakey was going to get worse and worse about things and keep riding his high horse till somebody took him down.

"Yummy, yummy," he said, giving the wisecrack back to his cousin. His mind was made up: If there was going to be trouble, then why prolong it? He stood directly in front of Jakey Darby, put his hands on his hips where he could get them up and in position if it came to that, and tried to find the right words.

"I don't know what you mean by that, but I think I know, and that's not the right way to start if we're going to be any kind of friends." Hogan wasn't aware how much he sounded like his father: calm, his words steady and to the point.

"I didn't ask to come here, you know, and all my friends are in Memphis . . ." Jakey started saying.

That was all Hogan needed to hear. He turned abruptly and started walking away, but not toward the other fields or the house. The dirt farm road that ran from the church to the house went by the house and curved north between the north field and a thick line of trees on the other side. It was toward that line of trees that Hogan walked, leaving Jakey behind him with one of three choices to make: stay where he was in the hot sun, go back to the house by himself, or run to catch up.

In a few moments he made up his mind and caught up. "Hey, that was pretty good. Corny, but pretty

good," he said. "I saw John Wayne do that in *Hondo*
. . . walk away from a fight. Alan Ladd did it twice in
Shane. You as tough as you act?"

Hogan stopped in the shade of an oak growing out
of the brake on the far side of the road and looked
again at his cousin. They were the same size and
roughly the same weight. Jakey was about an inch
taller and maybe five or ten pounds heavier, but top-
heavy and awkward. They both were still growing,
but Jakey looked like he was growing faster and
would end up being taller. It would be a good fight,
Hogan decided, and maybe a fight was called for.

"Why don't we find out who's the toughest?" he
said, and they started circling each other slowly.

"When we get back and they ask us what happened,
we've got to have a good reason," Jakey suggested. He
stepped back from the circling and quickly stripped
himself of his shirt.

That made sense and could save a lot of trouble.

"Let's just say we talked it over and wanted to
fight," Hogan suggested back.

"Fine with me," Jakey said. "Now who goes first?"

Whoever took the first swing would have the most
trouble later on.

"We'll flip for it" was Hogan's solution. He took
out a nickel and got it ready to flip. "Heads you take
the first swing; tails I do."

Jakey nodded, and Hogan sent the coin spinning
into the air. It came down heads, and Hogan bent over

and picked it up. Instead of straightening back up, though, he faked it, rising about halfway before ducking again and jumping sideways. Jakey's fist came zipping through the empty air where Hogan's head would have been, a roundhouse right. He was up then and dancing, jabbing three quick lefts into Jakey's defense and looking for an opening with his right. He created that opening by feinting a right toward his cousin's head, making him bring his left too high; stepping inside a possible right counter, he lowered his own right and rammed his fist into the unprotected stomach. It was a good blow, square across the knuckles with good weight behind it. It was a satisfying blow, but it didn't produce the results, the "ooof" that Hogan expected, and he admired it a little too long. The pain shot down the side of his head from a punch he truly didn't see coming and went straight to his knees, making them tremble and almost cave in.

But Hogan had been hit before and knew what to expect in a fight. It would take a few seconds for his head to clear, and to get those few seconds, he covered his head with his arms and crouched to protect his middle. He felt Jakey's fists on both his arms as Jakey searched for the connection that would end it. It had to be hurting Jakey's hands more than it was hurting his own arms, so he let his cousin make two more attempts. Then he straightened fully erect and threw his right forward from the shoulder, a straight shot that caught Jakey in the right side of his mouth and cheek. Jakey went down, and blood came flowing from the cut lips.

One way or another the fight was over. Hogan's right hand was numb and useless; in the next few minutes it was going to start swelling. Jakey's teeth were now bathed in blood, and another fist in the same spot would cost him a few teeth. Instead of Jakey's getting up, Hogan sat in the road beside him, so tired he wouldn't have cared much if a truck ran over him.

"What do you say we quit?" he offered.

"What do you say we flip another coin," Jakey came back, confusing him, "see who gets to quit first?" He spit a string of blood and watched it lump up in the powdery dust of the road.

They talked about the fight, then admitted that it was the best fight either of them had been in in years, each agreeing that the other was tough. Then up came Butterbean, reminding them that the world was still there, and they walked back to the house to face the music. Jakey had been in Louisiana exactly two hours and twenty minutes. It wasn't quite noon yet.

6: Facing
the Music

There was a cold-cut sandwich waiting for each of them when they came back from their "walk," and big glasses of RC and ice. They didn't have to explain what had happened; one look at the side of Hogan's head and his swollen fist, another look at Jakey's face and mouth told both sides of the story. The McGhees, Jakey discovered, believed in Dr. Tichenor's antiseptic for everything: busted lips, swelling, and bruising.

The three girls made the most of it, fussing over "poor Jakey" and calling Hogan, their own brother, a ruffian and common criminal.

"The human head," Gilbert McGhee finally said, after judging the results of the fight and declaring it something that was probably unavoidable, "is *too* hard to be pounding on with bare fists. The next time you two heathens want to go at it, let me know and we'll go over to the high school and use their gloves." Those turned out to be the only words—which to Hogan's mind was a miracle—that he ever said on the subject.

Grandma McGhee just looked at them and said, "Must have been a dilly."

Maybe it was kinship and heredity, and maybe it was the fight. What the family had expected to take longer to do had been done. The two kids were beaming, proud of themselves, and, when nobody was looking, actually grinned at each other and shook hands on their success. In a way it was like they weren't kids anymore, but grown-ups and friends for life.

7: The Discovery

Every discovery has an element of luck in it—sometimes good and sometimes bad—and making a discovery is a little bit like catching a fish. You could go fishing, you could have the right pole and the right bait and be on the right lake or river, the weather conditions might be perfect, and you still might not catch any fish. Like Hogan and Jakey, you've got to be in the exact right spot at the exact right time.

Hogan, Jakey discovered, had a weird sense of humor. When they set out again in the afternoon to look at the farm, not just look at it this time but explore it, Hogan was again the guide. This time, though, exploring the farm was more fun.

"Why in the world did our great-grandfather decide to build a farm and house right on the side of a swamp?" was one of Jakey's first questions.

They were walking up the road on which they'd had their fight, throwing rocks at trees growing out of brackish green water. The water was so thick that when the rocks missed the trees and landed in it, it didn't splash or make ripples.

"That's not a swamp," Hogan told him. "It's what we call a brake. That one's called Lemon Brake, and the Natches Bayou runs right through the middle of it. Tell me about the gang you hung out with in Memphis."

"Did you ever see the movie *The Blackboard Jungle?*" Jakey asked him. Hogan hadn't seen it because he didn't go to many movies, but he knew what it was about. "Well," Jakey went on, "there's gangs in that movie, and ever since it came out, people've been calling us a gang. We're a club. We pay dues and everything. I'm the secretary-treasurer, and I take care of all the money. When I had to quit going to meetings, we had over a hundred dollars."

"But you get in fights . . ." Hogan objected.

"We got in one fight, and that's because another bunch of guys from midtown, which is around Sears, told us we couldn't play in Overton Park anymore without kicking their asses." Jakey looked at the green, slimy, snake-infested water again and the trees, all hung with long, dusty tangles of Spanish moss. "This stuff good for anything?" he asked, pulling a beard off a low-hanging limb by the road.

"If it were good for anything, you think it would be hanging on all the trees? In the old days they used the bayous to travel on, like roads. When my father was growing up, he walked down to the bayou, and there was a boat that picked him up and took him to school. They had school boats instead of school buses. That's why the house is so close to everything." Hogan was surprising himself at how much he knew about the past. "In the old days they packed mattresses with that stuff." He took the moss from his cousin and worked out a brittle, sharp stem. "It wasn't very comfortable, and the only people who still use it are people like Pigiron." It was Pigiron, who lived in a shack beside the Natches, that they were going to see. "Pigiron's never bought anything in his whole life."

Ahead of them the road curved to the right, around trees. When the two boys got there, Jakey saw that these trees weren't in water, but they would be if the water level got any higher. Leaning against the barbed-wire fence were five or six long, pointed spears. The best of the spears was an old boat paddle, sharpened on one end and carved to a fork on the other.

"Whenever I go see Pigiron, I always carry a stick," Hogan told him. He chose the best stick for himself and handed Jakey the next best.

Jakey, about that time, was wondering if he really wanted to see anybody who lived in a swamp. He didn't want to think about *why* they needed big, heavy sticks, and the look on his face must have given him away.

"Pigiron's harmless," Hogan told him, laughing. "There's other things that're not so harmless, though, including Pig's dog."

Heading into the heart of the swamp, right where the road curved, was a fishing road—two ruts that a jeep or Willis might get down in good weather, but not much else, and it was down those ruts that Hogan clearly intended to go. The whole thing reminded Jakey of the kind of jungle and swamp movies he had seen where convicts or somebody on the run takes off for the swamps. The minute they go in you know it's a mistake because every snake that's in there knows they're coming and every tree has a wild Indian in it with a blowgun.

Down those dark ruts they started, with Hogan leading the way and Jakey, not sure at all about the situation, following.

The first thirty yards or so were okay. As long as you kept looking left, right, and behind you, nothing was going to rush up and surprise you. But right about forty yards, the ruts made a bend around a low, marshy area, with stagnant water and nasty, thick cattails on both sides of a suspicious-looking over-grown path. That path was so snaky-looking that even the brave Hogan slowed down and poked the bushes with his stick a few times before going farther. "You ready for an adventure?" he wanted to know. All Jakey could do was say yes.

That yes was the start of the longest two minutes

of his entire life. With caution—with *extreme* caution—he walked behind Hogan through that stand of cattails, ready with his pole to spear anything that came at him, concentrating on his feet and stepping as much as possible in the same tracks his cousin made.

"There's an alligator that lives in here we call Ole Smiley," Hogan whispered. "He chased me up a tree last month, and there was a dad-burned moccasin in the tree after birds' eggs. I had to break off a limb and get the snake before he got me, but it turned out to be a good thing. I knocked him out of the tree, and Ole Smiley took off after him. I was able to climb down and get away."

On the other side of the cattails, the path they were walking on got mushier and more narrow. The path was the dam that was keeping the stagnant bog on the right from joining the stagnant water on the left. One false step, and they'd be up to their knees in the stuff. Jakey was about to ask how anybody with a brain in his head could live in a place like this, but he never got the chance.

"There he is!" Hogan suddenly yelled, and there he was indeed. In the middle of the bog and coming at Jakey like a torpedo was an alligator, not one of your cute little lizard-sized alligators, but one as big as a log. The pole in Jakey's hand was suddenly too heavy to hold onto, something that would only trip him or slow him down. He was trying to get his feet off the ground so his arms could start flying, but they didn't want to move. His good friend and cousin Hogan McGhee had already taken off, running and laughing, leaving him there to die. It was an alligator, a real live alligator, swimming right at him.

When that thing raised its head out of the water and made a hissing noise, so close that Jakey could almost smell its breath, Jakey let loose a scream. That scream probably saved his life because all of a sudden his feet came unstuck. Up the path he went, putting thirty quick yards between him and what was after him, headlong through the cattails and ferns to the other side and up a slippery bank to safety.

He was back on the rut road, and he could see that the little detour they'd made had been staged for his benefit. Hogan was laughing so hard he couldn't even stand up. He was lying down between the ruts, holding his sides and kicking both his big feet in the air like a wild man.

"That mean old alligator scare you?" Hogan teased when he finally got his breath.

Jakey thought about it before he said anything. "I'll get you back for that, just as soon as I figure out what you did."

"What I did," Hogan told him, recovering and standing up, "was too easy. I couldn't resist it, and if you plan to get me back, join the waiting line. Half the people in town've been trying to get me back forever."

When Hogan explained how Old Smiley was Pig-iron's pet and not quite harmless, but not dangerous either, because he didn't have one of his front legs and couldn't get out of the water, Jakey had to laugh, too. "I could have had a heart attack," he said.

Pigiron's place wasn't like anything Jakey had ever seen before, in the movies or out. Twenty or thirty yards up the ruts from where they came out of the bog, around a curve where a person couldn't see it until they were in it, was a clearing, and flowing through that clearing to where it spread out and disappeared into the brake was the Natches Bayou. Hanging over the bayou from a couple of trees on one side to a couple on the other was a wobbly, uneven rope bridge like the kind Tarzan might make, if all he had to work with was different-sized pieces of rope and old boards. On the other side, sticking out over the water on stilts, was Pigiron's shack, and Tarzan wouldn't have lived in a place like that in a million years. Ma and Pa Kettle might, but not Tarzan.

Everywhere he looked, all Jakey could see was junk; the clearing on both sides was full of it. There were piles of junk under all the trees and hanging from the bridge. There was junk piled up in old junk cars and on top of them. There were piles of it stacked on old junk couches and chairs—every kind of junk you could imagine: old airplane propellers, rims from worn-out bicycles; pictures of horses that had been painted by numbers; catfish heads; rusted tools;

clothes that were nothing but rags that were hung on hangers; old shoes, boxes and boxes of them; vacuum cleaners; broken dishes; cans; magazines that had been swollen by rains; jars. . . .

"Pigiron," Jakey said matter-of-factly, "is crazy." He knew he was looking at something that no sane man would ever do. And it had been done; it didn't all get there by accident. What made it spooky, besides the mossy trees and the general darkness of the place, was that all the junk seemed to be arranged, like there was some purpose to it.

"Crazy as a loon," Hogan said, agreeing. "But since he's been living here, about five years, we haven't had one cow stolen. There's no way anybody's going to come on our place without Pigiron's knowing it. See that dog." Hogan was pointing to a huge, mean-looking gray and black splotched dog that was lying in the shade of the house, his white eyes watching their every move. "That's Benny, and if we started across that bridge without Pigiron's being here to stop him, he'd chew out both our livers. Even Ole Smiley's afraid of him."

Pigiron was out fishing, Hogan decided, because his boat was gone, and they wisely chose not to cross the bridge. There was something else Hogan wanted Jakey to see, the farm's old barn. It was in the field north of them so Hogan led them in that general direction on a path that ran along the bayou. On the way Hogan told him a story about how they'd hung a

Yankee in the barn and how you could still see the hanging rope tied to a rafter.

Jakey didn't believe it for a minute. The barn was old enough to have been in the Civil War, but the rope wasn't. Even Jakey's inexperienced eyes could tell that the stubby little piece of rope that was knotted around the rafter wasn't big enough, strong enough, or old enough to hold up a Yankee spy; moreover, he'd already learned to be suspicious of his good cousin Hogan McGhee.

The barn was so dilapidated that Jakey wondered what kept it up. Boards were missing out of all four walls, and vines, which looked like poison ivy vines, were almost as thick inside as they were outside. Whole patches were missing out of the tin roof, and birds had made nests in all the rafters. The birds had been in there longer than that rope.

"If that's a Civil War hanging rope, then I'm a Japanese general. In the first place, they didn't tie ropes to things like that; they tied them down low and looped them over limbs and rafters."

Hogan admitted that he wasn't *sure* the story was true. "It seemed like a good story when I made it up," he said. He knew the knot was there, and the story had leaped into his mind.

Jakey was already looking at something else.

Against the far wall of the barn, under the part that was still covered by some roof, was a hayloft. Hanging through the crack in the boards was a dark green canvas strap, and that's what Jakey was looking at. The strap wasn't actually hanging but had slipped through the crack sideways. Jakey was curious because it looked brand-new. An old canvas strap would have faded, but this one was so bright and new you could almost smell it.

Hogan looked at it, and it had him wondering, too. He got Jakey up on his shoulders so that he could reach it; Jakey pulled at it, but it was hooked onto something on the top, and the only way they knew to find out what it was was to get up there.

That took some doing, but they figured it out. First Jakey, again sitting on Hogan's shoulders, held onto the side of the loft while Hogan ducked out of the way; then, stage two, Hogan got his shoulders under Jakey's feet and boosted him high enough to swing a leg up.

"Watch out for snakes," Hogan warned him, and Jakey disappeared from view. In a few moments Hogan saw the strap slide back up through the crack. "What is it?" he yelled. There was more commotion in the loft, and old straw began filtering through the cracks.

"You're not going to believe this," Jakey called down. When he came to the edge again, in his arms he was holding a backpack and a camouflage fatigue cap with "USMC" stenciled across the front. The look on his face was like a kid's first Christmas. "You remember those marines that disappeared down in Houston?"

It was pretty hard to forget nine missing marines whom everybody in the world had been looking for.

"I think we just found their stuff," Jakey told him. He started handing down backpacks and other supplies, and Hogan began laying them out on the barn's dirt floor. When it was all down, there were nine backpacks laid out; the supplies were in two large cardboard barrels.

Jakey then followed, hanging from the loft and dropping to the ground.

Hogan was excited, but a little bit scared, too. "We've got to tell somebody about this," he said, but Jakey said no.

"Not on your life. The first thing we've got to do," he said, "is figure this out."

8: A Little G-2 Work

There was enough stuff in the backpacks to occupy the boys' minds for a little while. For the best part of the afternoon they studied and restudied, analyzed, and reanalyzed everything in the packs and barrels, trying to put together the clues and make some sense out of it. In the beginning, it was Jakey Darby who turned out to be the better detective.

Jakey knew more about the marines than Hogan, and that was because he was from Memphis. The Memphis papers and television had been full of missing marines stories because the men were from Millington, the big naval air station north of town. Jakey had even been up there once, with his class in school on a field trip. When you grow up in Memphis, you see Marines everywhere because they hang out in places like the zoo, the parks, and downtown. You couldn't go downtown without seeing jarheads.

He'd also seen about every Marine movie ever made, from *Gung Ho* to *Battle Cry*, which just came out last year. To see it, he'd had to hitchhike all the way downtown to the Malco and back, but it had been worth it. Army movies were good, but for some reason Marine movies were always better.

"You know what G-two is?" he asked. Then, without giving Hogan a chance to answer, he answered himself. "It's intelligence. Military intelligence. G-one is something like operations, and G-three is something else, like transportation. G-two is in charge of things like interrogating captured prisoners, watching out for spies, and trying to find out everything about what the enemy is doing."

"And what does the *G* stand for?" Hogan was asking a logical question, he thought, but Jakey got mad.

"Who cares what it stands for? In the military letters don't have to stand for anything; they can just be letters. *G* is just a letter, and the intelligence section is called G-two. It's in every movie they ever made. They catch a spy or get some prisoners, and they say 'Get them over to G-two.'"

"We got nine packs for nine men. We got extra clothes, socks, hats, and a bunch of other stuff. We got one hundred and thirty-five packages of dried food." He held up one of the packages from the barrels and showed it to Hogan for the fifth or sixth time. "Instant stuff. Dehydrated, powdered, and flaked. Instant coffee. Powdered milk. Flaked potatoes. Powdered eggs. Dehydrated macaroni and cheese." Each package was divided into three meals, a daily ration. In all, there was enough food in the barrels for nine men to live for fifteen days. He didn't analyze the clothes because they weren't as important. Clothes were clothes.

"So what?" Hogan said.

There was other equipment to consider, and Jakey had considered it all: sleeping bags that were thin, light, and easy to carry; compasses, knives, canteens. "They're walking," he said. "They're walking, and this is their resupply dump. It's been twenty days since they disappeared in Houston. If they weren't walking, they'd have been here by now. They're on their way here to pick this all up and go on somewhere else."

"Okay," Hogan said, "they're on their way here to pick it up and they're going somewhere else. Why's that so great?"

Jakey was never more sure of himself in his life and was already starting to stuff things back into the packs. "We've got to get all this stuff back like we found it," he announced.

"You want to tell me why?" Hogan didn't like to do anything without a reason.

"Don't you understand?" Jakey had to tell him. "They're on their way here. They're on their way here *right now*."

And all of a sudden it made sense.

Back up in the loft Jakey went, and back up went the supplies. By the time he got it all put back the way he found it, Hogan was starving to death. On their way back to the house they decided to keep their discovery to themselves, at least for one more day.

9: Charlie Chan and Sherlock Holmes

It was hard for Jakey to believe it was only his first day in Louisiana. So much had gone on, and there was still so much to do, he was sorry he'd put up such a fight about coming. Of course, he hadn't known then how much fun it could be; the only thing he'd known was that his mother was shipping him out to live with a bunch of country hick preachers. That night at supper he found out how unpreacherlike they were.

The McGhees had the worst table manners he'd ever seen in his life, worse even than the kids at his school. They said the blessing—his mother had told him to expect that—but they didn't pay any more attention to it than anybody else in the world. All the food was up toward the grown-ups' end of the table, and after they had filled their plates, Aunt Lucy began putting it down on their end. The only time the family passed food around was on Sunday. Uncle Gilbert had figured out that it took ten minutes longer to pass food around than it did just to grab what you wanted, and the food got cold before you got a chance to start eating it. It was Grandma McGhee, Jakey found out, who slowed everything down.

As soon as the food hit their end of the table, the girls and Hogan started grabbing it. Supper that night was steak—the McGhees had a whole freezer full of steaks, from cows they'd decided to eat themselves—mashed potatoes, corn on the cob, and homemade ice cream. Jakey was amazed at the way the food disappeared. There were five steaks, but by the time he learned to grab there was only one left to grab, the smallest. The same was true of the corn and the biscuits. He didn't get nearly as much of the potatoes as the others did.

And that wasn't the worst of it. The McGhee kids weren't just food hogs but food thieves as well. He had cut himself a prize square of steak, right from the middle of the lean. He was just about to pop it in his mouth when one of the girls, the one they called Glo, from Gloria, asked him to pass her the butter. When he looked back at his plate, the piece was gone, and he couldn't tell who had got it. The girls on both sides of him and Hogan all were chewing, and not one of them cracked a smile. From then on he watched his plate.

On an ordinary night, after supper and dishes, Hogan would listen to the radio for a while and read the junk his mother picked out for him. His mother made him read a real book a week all summer long, sometimes two, if he finished one too soon. This night, though, was special.

The McGhee house was a big house, with extra bedrooms and extra beds in all the kids' rooms. It was up to Hogan where Jakey would sleep: with him in the extra bed or in one of the other bedrooms. They didn't want to force Jakey on him if they weren't friends. As it turned out, both boys wanted to be together.

Hogan's father had some good road maps of Louisiana, Texas, and Mississippi, and Hogan took them to the room. That night they sat on the floor between the beds and studied them, checking at the door every few minutes to make sure none of the girls was spying.

They drew a line from Houston to the farm, along the route that looked the best for somebody walking who didn't want to be seen, and measured it. It came out to be around 265 miles if they measured right, and the line wasn't easy to measure because it circled a lot.

If Jakey was an expert on the Marines, Hogan was one on things that had to do with the great outdoors: hunting, fishing, camping, and, in this case, hiking. "People walk around three miles an hour, usually," Hogan said, "but that's when they're walking on roads and streets and they can see where they're going. Walking's a lot slower and harder when you're walking at night and when you're walking in the woods."

"Why at night?" Jakey asked him.

Hogan pointed to where the farm would be if the mapmakers had drawn it in. "All this open space between towns isn't really open. People live everywhere, like we do and Pigiron does. If they were walking in daylight, nine missing marines who everybody's looking for, how far do you think they'd have gotten?"

The answer to that was: not very far. As for how fast people could walk at night, the only thing to do was test it.

It wasn't unusual for the McGhee kids to be outside

at night in the summer, so nobody paid much attention to their going out to the porch.

"It's almost exactly a half mile down to the church," Hogan told him. "You walk down there and back, and I'll time you." It was a nice try, but it didn't work. They both walked to the church and back, and it took them twenty-four minutes, twelve minutes down there and twelve minutes back.

That figured out to be about two and a half miles an hour. Back in their room, the boys decided that the marines would be going even more slowly because of the backpacks, because some nights it would be raining, sometimes it would be uphill and downhill, neither of which is easy at night, and some nights they'd have to cross gullies and climb down cliffs and swim rivers and bayous.

Jakey was pretty sure they'd disappeared on the eighth of the month; that was twenty nights ago if Hogan was right and they were traveling at night. It was dark at around nine at night and light again at five in the morning; eight hours of walking at 2½, or say 2 miles an hour . . . 16 miles a night times twenty nights . . . that was 320 miles.

"They'd have been here already," Jakey said, "so they must be going slower."

"No." Hogan thought about it. "You can't walk eight hours a night steady; you've got to take time to rest and eat, and there'd be times when you just had to stop and hide from people. They'd be lucky if they've been making much over twelve or thirteen miles."

"If they did thirteen a night," Jakey said, the back of his neck tingling with the same excitement and urgency that he had felt in the barn, "they'll be here tonight."

"Or tomorrow night," Hogan said, yawning, "or the night after; or they might get caught on the way or drown in the Red River." It had been quite a day for him, too. His hand was sore, the side of his head was sore, and he was going to bed.

There wasn't anything for Jakey to do but follow suit.

PART TWO

The Partisans

10: Natchitoches, Louisiana, June 28, 1956

The adult human step is about one yard, and there are exactly 1,760 yards in a mile. According to Sims's calculations, then, he had already taken more than 400,000 steps on this trip. Before it would be over, he'd probably take another 120,000. The first thing he was going to do when all this was over was sit down and write a book. It was going to be all about walking, the physical step after step after step of walking.

All Groh could think about was cars: big ones, little ones, pink ones, and black ones. Not just normal cars like Fords and Chevies but big road lizards like New Yorkers and Caddies. He imagined cars with everything in them, with televisions, hard liquor bars, and

57

even beds. He thought about cars that were magic, where you could push buttons and they'd get big enough to live in, like house trailers, and little cars, like convertibles, that were so small that you could slip them on your feet like slippers. He was going to invent cars like that, cars that could do everything, so he'd never have to walk again.

Three-Finger Hopper had lost the two fingers when he was in the tenth grade; he'd been planing a board that was too short to be cut on the planer, using his naked hands. He would willingly have given up three years of Marine Corps pay to go back and change his own history. He wished he'd been planing the thing with his naked feet so there'd be less of them now to hurt.

Ross dreamed of being rich, of having enough money to hire somebody to do everything he didn't want to do. The next time they wanted somebody to walk 400 miles, he'd hire somebody that looked like him to walk in his place.

Turkey Jones was a philosopher. For the last 100 miles he'd been thinking about the meaning of life, and he'd just about figured it all out. Life didn't exist. It was all just a long dream, and since it was a dream, he was going to sleep. When all this was over, he was going to crawl in a bed somewhere and sleep till he died.

By the time they reached the barn that's all they could even think about, each and every one of them:

climbing into the hay and sleeping; pulling off their boots and smelly socks and sleeping. And that's what they'd all done, all except the one whose turn it was to be on guard duty. When the two boys came to explore the barn, that person had been Jenkins, the old house burglar, and Jenkins had heard them coming a mile away. He woke everybody up, and by the time the boys got there the squad had slipped out the back, through the loose boards, and were hiding in the swamp.

The two boys had left empty-handed, taking their time as though there had been nothing unusual in the barn. And indeed, when the squad moved back into the barn, their supplies were exactly the way they'd left them.

They made the necessary exchanges, and with fresh food in their packs, new clothes and boots, and new equipment, they prepared to move out. Their old stuff, including their old maps, they buried in the ground under the hay in the barn.

Sims made an entry in his journal that they'd successfully taken on fresh provisions and had been lucky in not being discovered. At 2145 it was dark enough to move out, and he went back to thinking about the book he was going to write.

11: It Begins for the Boys

At breakfast the next morning Jakey started grabbing food just as quickly as everybody else, and when somebody asked him to pass something, he kept one of his hands covering his plate. That made everybody smile, even old Grandma Mc-Ghee.

Not only was he already a part of the McGhee household, but he'd abandoned his city clothes for some of Hogan's. They both were now dressed alike, in dark green and dark blue T-shirts, jeans, and tennis shoes. Hogan and Uncle Gilbert liked wearing baseball caps to keep the sun off their faces, and they had one for him, a black one that said "Wayne Feeds" in front.

Jakey had suggested they wear the darkest clothes they could find. The marines' clothes had been camouflaged; if they were going to spy on them, theirs ought at least to be dark.

And that was, first of all, what Jakey had in mind.

Hogan, though, had morning chores. He had to look at and count 200 head of cattle. Looking at them meant looking at their hides to make sure they hadn't hurt themselves and watching them to see that they were eating. It usually took him about an hour and fifteen minutes, but with Jakey helping him and trying to go too fast, it took longer.

"If the marines are there," Hogan finally had to say, "they'll be there when we're done. If they're not, they won't be, and there's nothing we can do about it." On a feeder farm like theirs, the cattle always came first.

What Hogan didn't consider was a third possibility—that the marines had been there, gotten their stuff, and gone—but Jakey had considered it and was nervous. It did seem to him they could go check on the situation, then do the chores; cattle were dumb creatures and wouldn't know the difference.

When they got to the barn around midmorning, they found that the worst had indeed happened: The marines had come through sometime during the night and had given them the slip.

"I'm sorry," Hogan told him. And he was sorry, but he was also relieved. He expected Jakey to be sorry, too, and disappointed. But if he was, Hogan couldn't tell it; he walked out of the barn looking resigned to the situation, as if fate had pulled a trick on them, and sat down in the morning shade with his back against the barn.

"Let's just go tell my dad what happened and get him to call the sheriff," he suggested, but Jakey didn't want to do that.

"And then what happens?" Jakey said, shaking his head. "They come out here and look and they don't find anything, and we look like all the other loonies that've been saying they saw them."

"Maybe they left something." Hogan sat down and

shrugged. "Seems to me like we ought to do something."

"That's it!" Jakey suddenly yelled, jumping to his feet. "They would have taken the food and the other stuff, but why take old dirty clothes? They'd have hidden that stuff somewhere." He closed his eyes and tried to think of what he'd have done if he were a marine.

The air was filled with some kind of weed that made him want to sneeze. With his eyes closed he could smell the cattle, and he could smell something rotten, which he figured was the swamp. There was a sweet smell someplace, not like anything he'd ever smelled in Memphis. In Memphis by this time of the morning the trucks took over, or the Wolf River that got all the crap from Humko.

If they had hidden stuff, they wouldn't take a chance on people finding it by accident. They'd have put it in something, weighted it down with rocks, and sunk it in the swamp, or they would have just dug a hole right there in the barn and buried it—that would have been the easiest and the safest because there were people like Pigiron who might see or hear them sink it.

"Let's take another look inside," he said. When they took the second look, there was a place where straw looked rearranged.

It hadn't been buried deep, and it was all there: the marines' old dirty clothes, the worn-out equipment, their garbage—all the evidence they needed to call the sheriff or police. And that's what they were going to do till Jakey went through the pants and shirt pockets. In the shirt pocket with the name "JONES" stenciled above the pocket he found a hand-drawn map.

It wasn't much more than lines and numbers, but there were a few words: barn, park, cutoff, ditch, and tracks. The words made sense to Hogan, and the numbers made sense to Jakey.

Hogan had hunted, fished, hiked, and generally lived in the area too long not to recognize it on a map, even such a crude map as the one he was looking at. "Here's the barn," he said, pointing to a dot. "And here's our road, and here's the St. Maurice Cutoff." The cutoff, he explained, was the old road to Winnfield, used long before he was born. "It's gravel, and not many people live on it because it's in the national forest." It was the best way for the marines to have gone.

The map had been drawn on a piece of notebook paper, the kind from a spiral binder, ragged on the edge. Hogan thought the numbers were in code till Jakey recognized what they were. What the mapmaker had done was put down times the way the military wrote them—2330, for instance. From 0100 to 1200 was from one in the morning till noon. 1300 was 1:00 P.M. and 2400 was midnight, so 2330 was 11:30 at night.

M stood for miles, and if Hogan was right about the roads' being what he said they were, if the map was right about the distances and the times, if everything they had figured out together was right, they knew exactly which way the marines had gone and where they'd be camped for the day.

"I could take us right to them," Hogan said, not really meaning they should give it a try. But Jakey took him seriously, jumping up from the ground where he was sitting and dancing in circles like a heathen.

If they had really wanted to turn the missing marines in and get the credit for doing it, they could've done that yesterday. But that was like squealing, Jakey insisted, and the worst thing you could be was a squealer. There wasn't any glory in it, and it wouldn't be much fun. The fun would be in catching up with them and figuring out what they were doing. When Jakey wanted to argue for something, Hogan learned, it was hard to argue against it, and Hogan gave in.

The plan they came up with was simple enough to work like a charm. When they got back to the house, they found everybody getting ready for a trip into town—everybody except Grandma McGhee, who was talking on the phone to her girl friend and wouldn't be through for hours. Hogan asked his father for permission to take the bikes and go camping over in the ranger district and got it. In the state of Louisiana, Jakey learned, a lot of things were called by different names from those in other states: A swamp was a brake, a county was a parish, and a national forest was called a ranger district. Permission was given, with the only stipulation that they be back in time to take baths, get presentable, and go to church with the rest of the family on Sunday. Jakey was going to be presented and get welcomed by the congregation.

Jakey cringed at the thought.

"And sweet little Kathy Bender will be there," the girls teased. Hogan had mentioned once that Kathy Bender was the prettiest girl in church, and his sisters hadn't let him forget it.

The bikes were the kind that had three speeds, big balloon tires, and baskets on the front big enough to hold newspaper sacks. There was camping equipment in the new barn: sleeping bags and a two-man pup tent, cooking and mess kits, old army surplus raincoats, and backpacks. Hogan and his father did a lot of hunting and camping, fishing mostly. The cousins decided to take a hatchet for firewood and some fishing line and hooks, just in case they needed them. All the equipment fitted nicely into the backpacks, except the knife and hatchet, which they wore on their belts with canteens.

The only thing left to do was get the maps and pack the food.

Grandma McGhee was still on the phone when they made their food run and hardly knew they were in the house. They'd rolled the bicycles around to the back porch and put an ice cooler in one basket and a cardboard box in the other. First they made sure that Grandma McGhee was still talking; then they raided the pantry and freezer.

In the pantry there were shelves full of vegetables, fruits, and jellies, all in glass canning jars that had stick-on labels that were signed by one of the three girls or Aunt Lucy and dated: creamed corn, pickles, beans of all kinds, tomatoes, peaches, and pears. Half the jars had red, white, or blue ribbons on them from county and state fairs as far back as 1950. Raiding that pantry was just like raiding a little grocery store.

From the freezer they decided to take steaks, since steaks were the right size for cooking and eating, and no matter what you did to them they'd still taste good. Five apiece, they figured, ought to do the trick.

Matches to light the campfires. A candle so they could see at night. Ice for the ice chest to keep the meat from spoiling.

They had one false start. They were on the road to the church, still close to home, when Hogan remembered his father's binoculars and made the mistake of asking Jakey if he thought they might need them. It wasn't hard for Jakey to answer because there were few things in life he wanted more than a good pair of field glasses. His father had brought a pair home from

Germany but had sold them to somebody or traded them away.

Hogan went back for them while Jakey held the bikes; after that it was on to Winnfield.

12: The First Day

The riding of the bicycles turned out to be harder than Jakey thought. Not only was the afternoon hot, but there was something about riding on a gravel road that made it seem even hotter. They could smell the dust when there wasn't any to smell, hardly, and when a car passed them and stirred it up, it almost choked them out. Because they were loaded down the way they were, it was impossible to pump up the hills and no fun to ride down them, since one false move would wipe them out.

On the very first hill, which they hit after getting on the St. Maurice Cutoff, they had to get off and push. Pushing was slow, and the stuff in the baskets weighed a ton.

"We probably shouldn't have worn all these dark clothes," Hogan said, and Jakey was tempted to agree with him but didn't. The sun was against them now, but it wasn't going to stay up forever.

They got over the first hill, which wasn't very high,

and ahead of them was a bigger one, which looked as if it might go on forever. "When we get up this one," Hogan told him, "we'll be out of the Red River Valley."

"You mean, 'from this valley you tell me we're leaving'?" Jakey couldn't resist asking. He thought he was being clever, but Hogan had heard it all before . . . about a million times.

The road became more rolling than steep once they were on top. There was more shade because they were in the national forest; on both sides of the road was forest as far as the eye could see, which wasn't very far because of the dusty vines and undergrowth. This part of Louisiana wasn't a lot different from Tennessee.

They were headed northeast for the first six miles or so. Except for the two cars that had passed them it had been quiet the whole way, their bikes and their talking being the loudest sounds they could hear. Then, in the last half mile, they could hear the traffic from 84, the big highway Jakey had come from the train station on. When it seemed that the dirt road they were on might cross it, theirs turned more in a due east direction, and Hogan got off his bike.

According to the marines' map, this was the place where the squad intended to rest and eat. The boys scouted the area closely and found where the marines had left the road; there were broken vines and tree limbs to show the way, and inside the cover of the trees there were signs where they had made a quick camp. The thick buzzing flies had found the make-shift privy, warning the boys where not to walk.

What had taken the marines three hours to reach, they'd reached in a little over two, and finding the spot meant some good things. It meant, first of all, that the map was accurate, even if it was only hand-drawn; it meant the marines had followed it and done what they intended to do; and most important, it meant they would find them camped in a ravine east of the railroad junction below Winnfield.

The next five miles were east again along the northern rim of the forest, but there was one dip south and around a ridge that cost them an extra mile. The marines, according to the map, had gone straight over the ridge and picked up the road again on the other side. Two more miles east, and the boys came to a place where they decided to stop and eat.

They were on a lookout point, though dumping point would be a better name for it, on top of a forty-foot bluff. People had been dumping their trash over the side recently, and it spoiled the view. They decided not to take the time to cook yet and instead opened a jar of canned peaches. "Could you climb down this bluff on a rope?" Hogan asked, slipping a peach half in his mouth and letting it slide down his throat like a little fish.

Jakey looked over the side, and it didn't look that tough.

"That's what the marines did," Hogan said, showing Jakey the map and the marines' notes. "They climbed down between oh-two-hundred and oh-two-fifteen, crossed the creek at the bottom, and filled their canteens." What the boys had to do was go a mile north of where they were, staying on the road, then come a mile back to the bridge they could see across the gorge from them. It would be a two-mile detour for them, but almost all downhill, for which Jakey was grateful.

His bones were beginning to ache, and he leaned his back against a rock and closed his eyes. He felt as far away from everything as he'd ever been in his life—away from Memphis and away from everything that Memphis meant: his mother fussing over him, school, his friends, homework, and problems. He also felt like he was away from Louisiana: his cousins, aunts, and uncles, the farm his mother had grown up on. . . . The fact that Hogan was with him didn't matter. Hogan could be his witness when he told about all this. There weren't many movies where the hero didn't have a sidekick or a costar who knew what the story was and made sure it was true.

When he got back to Memphis and told the story of how he'd tracked the missing marines partway across the state of Louisiana, they'd say he was lying. That's when he could say, "Put up your money and bet me, and I'll call the guy in Louisiana who went with me. I'll even pay for the call."

Hogan was thinking about something else entirely. He was thinking about what they were going to do when they caught up with the marines, as they almost surely would do in a couple of hours. He didn't know where they were going, or why; all he knew was that he was riding a bicycle full of food, carrying camping equipment on his back, tired as hell, with the sun not getting any cooler.

The question he was asking himself, if he put it into real words, was the eternal question that anybody with any sense might ask in his situation, looking down in a gorge at somebody's old bread wrappers, milk cartons, and tennis shoes: Just what, exactly, am I doing here?

He had the question but not the answer.

And they didn't stay there long. It took some careful steering around holes and washouts, but in a half hour they were on their bikes at the bottom of the gorge, looking back up at the top.

"We've got about four miles from here before we turn off on the tracks. If we're lucky, we've got only two miles of tracks." Hogan said this, looking at the hand-drawn map. It had been right so far; there was no reason to suspect it was wrong now. At the end of the two miles of tracks there ought to be a junction where a north-south line, probably the Kansas City and New Orleans, crossed. South of that junction 100 yards was a dry gully where the marines planned to camp.

"Why do you say 'lucky'?" Two miles or five miles, it didn't seem likely that either of them might be hit by a train, but maybe there was something about railroad tracks that Jakey didn't know.

"You'll find out," Hogan said, and five minutes after hitting the tracks Jakey did.

It was impossible to ride the bikes on them, and it was some of the hardest work he'd ever done in his life just to push them. Every crosstie was a bump, and every bump had to be gotten over. Thankfully there were only two miles to go on the tracks . . . thankfully and luckily.

Ahead of them they saw the junction, and they rolled their bikes down the steep sides of the tracks and hid them. Then, with Hogan showing Jakey what to do and take, they worked their way back inland and to the south toward some high ground in the trees, where they pitched the pup tent and made camp.

They had to do that while there was still light. Hogan started a fire while Jakey took the field glasses and climbed a tree to look for the gully.

When Jakey came back, from the look on his face everything they'd done—pushing the bikes, sweating in the sun, eating dust, getting blisters, and rubbing raw patches on their tails—was all worth it. There is a kind of glee a person takes at doing something well and being right, and Jakey Darby had that glee. Deep in his heart, Hogan didn't much care about the marines one way or another and wouldn't have followed them five feet if it hadn't been for Jakey. Now it was all worth it for Hogan, too.

The gully was only a little bit away—Jakey guessed about two city blocks—and the marines had a lookout under a bush. Jakey had actually seen him when he moved.

Hogan had put a couple of steaks on the fire to let them start cooking. He took them off and put them back in the ice chest to keep animals from stealing them and said, "Well, let's go see them critters."

13: Winnfield, Louisiana, June 29, 1956, 2020

Sims didn't have to open his eyes to know that it was almost time to start walking again. He could feel the sun fading through his closed eyelids. Sleeping through a day as hot as that one had been, in a dry, dusty ditch, was something ordinary people wouldn't have been able to do, but then ordinary people didn't walk all night under thirty-pound backpacks. He could probably have slept even longer, but Groh was pulling on his big toe.

"Blister check," Groh whispered. The first thing they did before starting a night's walk was take care of their feet. Sims opened his eyes then and watched Groh paint the back of his heels with an oily chemical called Tough-Skin.

"Peterson's got the fungus and won't let me spray his toes . . . says it burns," Groh reported, still talking in a whisper. All their talking had been in whispers since they'd left Houston.

Groh's telling on Peterson was as close as he ever came to a medical report. The two were actually good friends; only they liked persecuting each other.

"Tell him to spray his toes," Sims whispered, yawning, "or I'll cut the damn things off."

Peterson was close enough to hear for himself what Sims said; Groh tossed him the can of disinfectant and grinned.

The next two items on the agenda were eating and briefing, which they did at the same time. The ditch they were in was in the middle of a thorny thicket about thirty yards from the tracks they'd walked there on. On the maps that Jones was studying the ditch would get deeper and become a ravine a half mile farther south; where they were, though, it was just a ditch, and Russell was sitting on its sandy bottoms, boiling water on his burner for the squad's chow.

Sims pulled on his socks and boots and got his mess

kit out of his pack, along with that evening's breakfast: a package of dehydrated food with powdered eggs in one compartment, powdered potatoes in the other, a strip of dried beef, and enough granulated instant coffee to make two strong cups. The dried beef, of course, he ate dry; the rest of the food he handed to Russell, who mixed it in tin cups and tumbled it back on his plate as something like scrambled eggs.

It was as sad a breakfast as you'd ever want to see. The eggs were a color that was grayish green and were almost too terrible to choke down. The potatoes looked something like real mashed potatoes, but they had the taste and texture of globs of white wallpaper paste.

"When I was on watch, I smelled somebody cooking steak," Three-Finger Hopper said, wistfully remembering that people still ate steak, and wishing he had some. Others had smelled it, too, but hadn't said anything. The squad was long past the point of complaining about their food, and thinking about things like steaks was only painful.

Jones was through studying his maps and started drawing the route for them on his note pad. He drew a little line that was supposed to be their ditch in the lower-left-hand corner; then he drew a wiggly line in the upper-right-hand corner and a little arc over it to represent that night's destination.

"Okay," he started, pointing at the marks in the upper corner, "we're looking for a bridge over a place called Flatt Creek, exactly one and a half miles east of Sikes." With the squad looking on, he drew a square and wrote "Sikes" over it. "Population about seven thousand. The whole walk tonight will only be thirteen point eight miles, but Sarge wants us to have a wet camp, and the water in Flatt Creek looks good."

He went on with the details of the walk; when they left the ditch, they'd get on the railroad tracks and stay on them for nine and a half miles—he drew the tracks on his map for them. "At mile eight we cross a railroad bridge over Beech Creek. We'll stop and fill our canteens." A little over a mile past Beech Creek, they'd leave the tracks and head east on a country road. In three-quarters of a mile, they'd come to a church and cemetery and hit another country road, which would take them northeast. Within three miles from the cemetery they'd hit their target and camp north of the bridge.

Sims looked at Jones's map and made his decision. "We'll stop to eat when we stop for water."

It was going to be an easy night, good footing and the moon setting a little after midnight. They could probably make more miles; but the eighteen they'd walked the night before had put them ahead of schedule, and that wasn't necessarily good.

They cleaned up their mess and buried the garbage, including Jones's hand-drawn map. It was dark enough for them to start walking.

14: The Toughest
and the Meanest

When they saw the lookout crawl back down in the gully and nobody come out to replace him, they decided to crawl closer. From thirty or forty yards below the marines' position, with Jakey watching with the binoculars through a clump of dry weeds, they saw and heard that night's briefing. Jakey watched a tall marine, the one who was doing all the writing and talking, rip the page he was writing on from the notebook, crumple it, and bury it with the garbage, and he understood how they had made their first mistake. In a real war the Gestapo would have had their asses. So would the KGB. The only safe thing to do with something like a map is to burn it or eat it. You couldn't take it with you, because if you were caught, they'd have the whole squad.

Ten minutes after the squad had gone, the boys had that map back at their own campsite, looking at it with the flashlight.

"There's no way I'm going to push that bike over nine more miles of tracks," Hogan said flatly. "It's dark. I'm tired. I've gone as far as I'm going." He didn't know what Jakey had in mind, but he wasn't taking any chances.

"They were something, weren't they?" Jakey said, his eyes still seeming to see them, crouched at the briefing, all of them with their faces dark, two of

them eating with nothing but the tips of their bay-
onets. They hadn't been the kind of marines who
hang out in the parks and zoos. Those guys knew
what they were doing.

"They looked pretty tough," Hogan admitted. He
put the steaks back on the fire and started cooking
them. One of the jars in their canned food supply was
full of small onions in some special kind of garlic
sauce. He opened that jar and poured some of the
onions and sauce over the steaks. The resulting aroma
was almost heavenly.

"Tough?" Jakey laughed. In Memphis there was an
expression you used for the toughest and meanest.
"They'd have cut your fingers off for a nickel. Marines are the best there is, and those guys were the
best of the best." He went on and on about the marines and everything they had done and all the things
they could do while he and Hogan ate supper.

"If they're so good," Hogan finally had to ask, "how
come they ran away? And if they didn't run away,
how come the rest of the marines and the FBI and
everybody in the world are looking for them?"

That Jakey didn't know, but he did know one thing.
Marines didn't run away. They followed orders because following orders was beaten into their heads;
they didn't even have a choice about it. If they'd left
Houston, it was because they had orders telling them
what to do. They were on their way somewhere to do

something . . . practicing for a real war assignment, testing defenses, or anything.

It was still too hot to sleep in a tent. Hogan unrolled his sleeping bag and stretched out on it on the ground. The second star in the handle of the big dipper was a double star, he told Jakey. They looked at it through the binoculars, and true, it was.

An owl hooted in a tree somewhere, and they lay listening to it. After a while it either got tired of hooting or flew off to another part of the night.

Jakey's bones felt like rubber; there wasn't a part of his body that wasn't tired or sore except his mind. His mind was still working on those two questions: where and why? Where were they going and why? He started to say something to Hogan, but Hogan wasn't going to be listening. He'd put down the binoculars and was snoring.

15: On to Sikes

Where and why? Jakey had tried those two questions from every angle he could think of. He couldn't say for sure; but he felt like he'd tried them all night in his sleep, and he was stumped. They could be on their way to anywhere, for any reason, and there were only two ways to find out: follow them till they got to where they were going, or walk right up to them and ask.

Following them till they got where they were going didn't seem likely, not with a few jars of canned vegetables and peaches and four steaks apiece. Asking them directly seemed the only logical thing to do, and that's what he decided to do. He didn't tell Hogan his plan because he'd been watching Hogan as they broke camp that morning, and Hogan was just about ready to turn back.

"We're out of ice," Hogan said, looking at the cooler.

If they didn't get more ice, the eight steaks would spoil. That alone might have been enough to make Hogan want to go home unless Jakey acted quickly.

"We know where they are," he said as a matter of fact. "Why don't we push back over to the road, ride on up to Sikes, and get ice, then ride out to where they're hiding and spy on them one more time?"

"What then?"

Jakey had to think fast and say the right thing. "If it's like last night and they just go on, we'll camp and do a little fishing in the creek, get up early in the morning, and ride back in time for church."

When he said "fishing," he said the right word, and Hogan bought it, hook, line, and sinker. Hogan would make a good marine, Jakey decided; he was tough, easy to talk into things, and not too smart.

They made breakfast out of warmed vegetables, mostly creamed corn, and broke camp. The road through Winnfield and into Sikes was blacktopped and a hundred times easier on their legs and bikes than the one from the farm to Winnfield. They'd also gotten an early start, so the sun wasn't hot.

Riding into Sikes, they took their time, with Hogan explaining all the different parts of town. The first part they came to was the shotgun houses, where people lived who spent about half of their time working at farming a few acres and the other half working in town. The houses, which were almost always white, were called shotguns because they were long and skinny, never more than one room wide, with a door at the front and a door at the back. They all had big, well-kept gardens, taking up most of one side and half the backyard, and turkeys, pigs, and sometimes mules running around on the other side. There was always a butane tank and a chicken house somewhere and chickens and people roosting on the front porch.

The next part they passed was what Hogan called the red-knuckle district, which was closer to town. In this district people didn't farm so much as they worked on cars and trucks and washing machines or things with motors that were broken in their driveways and front yards. In almost every yard there was a car or truck with its hood up, its motor out on the oil-soaked grass.

Then they came to the business that took up a lot

of room, the big, square buildings made out of green aluminum that didn't have any windows and sold such things as fertilizer and irrigation pipe and car and tractor parts.

Then they came to the squatty-body buildings of downtown and passed what Hogan pointed out as the town's main industry besides farming, the saw and pulp mills—one mill that cut trees into lumber and one that made little trees into what would become paper. Neither of them smelled too good, but neither smelled as bad as pigs either. By the time they were all the way downtown Jakey knew as much about life in rural America as he wanted to know. "One of these days," he told Hogan, "you've got to come let me show you around Memphis." He smiled to think of how he could get Hogan back for Ole Smiley in Memphis.

Hogan didn't feel as bad the second day on the trail as he had the first, partly because he could now see the end and partly because he was in better shape than he'd realized. If his hand hadn't still hurt from the fight and his shoulders weren't sore from the backpack, he'd even feel good. He knew where there was a bait shop that sold a bit of everything—bait, groceries, gasoline, whatever anybody needed to go fishing—and they rode the bikes to it.

The bait shop was air-conditioned, which was nice, and the owner had a whole wall of the store devoted to cold drinks and beer. Jakey had five dollars in his pocket from the money his mother had given him to ride the train on, so they had money for drinks, cinnamon rolls, crickets, and ice. They stayed in the air conditioning for a long time, and Jakey watched a man in a green uniform start refilling the beer cases. Hogan bought another Coke, but Jakey went outside to check the air in his bicycle tires.

It was a short, bald-headed man who ran the bait shop, and he looked like a fisherman, so Hogan asked him about Flatt Creek. There were fish in it, the man assured him, perch and catfish, so Hogan bought a package of cornmeal to cook them in. If he or Jakey caught any, he'd cut off some steak fat and make some grease. Fresh-caught fish, rolled in cornmeal and pan-fried on an open fire, was about the best-tasting thing in the world.

When he came out of the bait shop, Jakey was already on his bike and ready to go. Hogan noticed that he'd taken his sleeping bag out of his backpack and had it folded in the basket around the box of food.

"Keep it from rattling so much," he said, and they started riding. In about ten minutes they'd put Sikes behind them on the road east toward the creek.

When they started getting close, Jakey slowed, and Hogan rode up alongside. It had been too dangerous to ride side by side near town because you never knew when some joker was going to come flying around a curve and wipe you out.

"When we get to the creek, I'll spot them out and see where they're holed up," Jakey offered.

"Fine with me," Hogan agreed.

"Then you can start fishing," he suggested, and that was okay, too, and they started riding again. In a few more minutes they came to a hill overlooking a creek and a one-lane bridge. They pulled their bikes off to the left side of the road, and Hogan handed Jakey the binoculars, saying, "Go to it, hero."

In the next few minutes Jakey worked himself carefully through the woods to a vantage point on the downslope toward the creek. Lying on his stomach under a bush, he began to search the area around the bridge, looking for a guard, suspecting that like the day before, they'd have one out.

And there he was, halfway up a tree by the bridge, so hidden in the leaves that Jakey wouldn't have seen him had he not reached up to wipe the sweat off his face and set a big crow flying. He still couldn't see where the other eight men were hiding, but it would have to be close, probably along the creek on the north side of the bridge.

Seeing the guard in a tree gave Jakey an idea, and he eased back over the hill to where he'd left Hogan with the bicycles.

"Okay," he said, squatting down and drawing the layout in the dirt. "The guard's up a tree, and the rest of them are along here." He drew lines for the stream, road, bridge, and tree. "If we come riding down the road on our bikes, he won't know whether or not we're planning to stop, so he'll take a chance that we're going to keep going. He's probably watched a dozen cars pass and keep going, so why not bikes? We'll freeze him in the tree. Then I'll keep him up there while you go fishing."

"But that's not like spying on them, that's like *catching* them, and you said you didn't want to catch them."

That was true, Jakey admitted. "But now you're about ready to get back, so let's find out what they're up to."

Hogan smelled a rat, but he couldn't quite tell what it was.

16: Caught!

It doesn't matter how good you are at something; do it long enough and often enough, and you're going to make a mistake. Acrobats fall off high wires, cowboys fall off horses, and ballplayers make errors; if it were easy and there weren't any way to make a mistake, it wouldn't be worth doing. Sims knew that, and so did the men, and they'd all tried to do everything the professional way—clean, sharp, without any complications.

But it's hard to do when you're tired, and Sims could see the tiredness creeping in. He'd warned them more than once to cut out the slop and even written about it in the journal he kept: "The real trouble is, we're not at war and the men know it. If we were, everything would be easier because problems take care of themselves. When you're trying to stay alive, nobody has to tell you to be careful . . . either you are or else you aren't . . . period." In spite of his warnings, the mistake was made when the boys found their old equipment and the maps. When the results came, Sims was asleep.

It was poor Lofton who was in the tree, Lofton, who liked to climb trees and sit in them for hours because it was a nice, different way to see things without anybody ever really seeing you. When the two boys came riding the bicycles down the hill toward where he was, he had no reason to believe that they'd stop or, worse, that they'd lean their bikes against the very tree he was in. There was nothing he could do but keep still and hope.

Directly below his limb, one of the boys took out a fishing line and some hooks and bait. He walked across the road and down to the creek, south of the bridge, thank goodness; the other boy started emptying the bike baskets and setting up a camp in the clearing under his tree. He set up a tent, unrolled sleeping bags, and rolled rocks together to make a campfire; then he opened a big metal ice chest on the ground there under the tree, and Lofton couldn't believe what the kid did next. He took out eight of the biggest, thickest, most beautiful sirloin steaks he'd ever seen in his life and stacked them up. Lofton thought he was going to lose his grip on the limb; his fingers and arms had almost gone numb.

If that were the end of it, he might have been okay. But it wasn't. The kid had a case of beer stuck down in one of the sleeping bags, and when he pulled it out and started loading it into the ice chest, can by can, already cold, for there were frost beads running down the sides of the cans, Lofton had to clamp down with his teeth on the tree to keep from whimpering.

Lofton saw what the kid was going to do. He tore up the cardboard beer carton and put it in the circle of rocks; then he started finding wood for a campfire. That little kid was going to cook those steaks and drink that beer right before his very eyes. He knew what the kid was going to do and he knew what he was going to do.

Private First Class Thomas J. Lofton was about to climb down from his tree and commit murder.

But as it turned out, he didn't have to. His relief on watch was Jenkins, and he could see Jenkins coming up the bank of the creek. There was no way to warn him, so he just sat tight. Jenkins wasn't the kind to leap before he looked where he was leaping. If he were, he'd have been dead a long time ago.

Jenkins knew something was wrong before his head cleared the top of the bank, and quickly moving to the right a few yards, he just peeked over from behind a bush. One look told him everything—not that there was beer in the cooler or how many steaks there were, but that there were two bicycles and probably two boys, though he'd seen only one, and that they were starting a fire and planning to spend the night, and one of the boys was the one he'd seen at the barn two days ago.

But that didn't make any sense.

Still puzzled, he climbed back down the bank and slipped silently upstream to where the rest of the squad were sleeping and shook Sims awake.

By the time Sims opened his eyes and focused them Jenkins was already writing notes on his note pad for Sims to read: "Lofton in tree. 2 bicycles under it. Sleeping bags, campfire. Only one boy. Same boy as at barn."

Sims didn't move. He just lay back on the ground and tried to think it through calmly.

Somewhere he knew they'd made a mistake, but he couldn't think of what it might have been. It could have been anything, and if it hadn't been one thing, it would have been another.

He lay there with his eyes closed and tried to think of a plan that might work, but all he could think about was the mistakes that people made. The more he thought about it, the more he believed that there was really only one mistake, and that was learning to walk. Babies do everything to learn how to walk: They hold onto the sharp corners of coffee tables; they pull themselves up with TV knobs; they grab tablecloths. If they're not bashing in their heads or falling down steps, they're burning themselves in the kitchen.

But if they never learned to walk at all . . . It was a silly thing to be thinking about, and he had to open his eyes to make himself quit. On the sheet of paper Jenkins had written the question "Wait till dark?" and was about to write "Run for it?" when they started smelling steak and onions cooking.

One by one the other five men in the squad began to stir in their sleep and open their eyes. The smell was too real to be a dream.

They were all in the hurried process of putting on their socks and boots when Lofton came walking into camp with a smile on his face, beer in one hand, and a mess kit skillet full of steak in the other one.

"We've been caught," Lofton said to the astonished faces looking at him. Then he sat on a log and started eating.

17: The Partisans

It had been Jakey's intention to offer the missing marines the only thing they had to offer—food—for information. Then he'd seen the opportunity to steal the case of beer from the beer truck, and he'd planned it and timed it and pulled it off. That was something that only a person like him, from the city, could do, and it all had turned out rather well. Tempting them out of their hiding places hadn't really occurred to him till he'd spotted the lookout in the tree.

There was enough cover around Jakey's fire for the squad to hide from any car or truck that might be passing, so they all came out. Lofton suggested they take their mess kits, and they did. There were eight men, and only seven steaks left, so they made an eighth one by cutting a little off the others. When everybody had had a beer and was on his second one, Jakey explained how he and Hogan had followed them, how they'd found where they buried their stuff in the field, how they'd found the first map and watched to see where they buried the second one. That was the big mistake the squad had made, leaving the maps instead of eating them.

Hogan came back with two bream and three white perch, none of them bigger than his hand, on a forked willow branch he was using for a stringer. He came walking up as Jakey was telling the amazed marines about all the news they had been making: newspapers, radio, and television.

"Not to mention everybody who's looking for you," Hogan put in. "Every police and sheriff's department in the whole country and the FBI."

The idea that the FBI was seriously looking for them and hadn't been able to find them pleased the men in the squad a great deal but only produced groans from Sims. Marine Corps, police, FBI—by the time he got out of jail he was going to have a long white beard and skin like a plucked chicken.

When Hogan just came right out and asked them where they were going and why, he beat Jakey to the punch by about two seconds, and the real answer didn't come close to measuring up to the Hollywood answers they had come up with.

"We're a demonstration unit," Sims said. "It's our job to make the Marine Corps look good, and we do that by doing what they tell us: march in parades; hang up flags in the morning; take them down at night. That's where we are now, on our way to hang up a flag and march in a parade." Sims did his best to explain their duties in language kids could understand.

"Then why are they looking for you?" was Jakey's next question.

"Because somebody made a mistake," Sims said. "Let me explain what I mean." Sims told them about a guy named O'Neil who was told to go home and wait for the sergeant to call him. "The guy was sitting at home for two and a half years. When he came back on his own, they couldn't do anything to him but give him his discharge papers, because he was only following orders."

When he told the two kids what he was doing, it made more sense than when he told himself.

"Our orders told us to report to a recruiting officer in Houston and take part in a recruiting demonstration. That's what we did. The mistake in our orders was that they said and gave the dates for June fourth through June eighth; Monday through Friday. Then they said we were then to proceed to our next assignment, where we were to report to another recruiting office, where we would perform a morning flag-raising service and march in a Fourth of July parade. Our orders told us exactly when to leave Houston, but not when to report to our next assignment. We think there was somebody new in Headquarters Division, and he didn't know how to write orders."

"So that's what we're doing," Groh, the former medic, piped in, "proceeding to our next assignment . . . only we're proceeding by walking."

Hogan was getting hungry, and the fish had been out of the water awhile now, so he started cleaning them.

"Let me do that," Peterson asked him, holding out his hand for Hogan's good cleaning knife. It had been years since Peterson had had the pleasure of cleaning fish, and he'd once done it all the time.

Jakey was trying to decide whether or not he believed their story. It sounded a little like something they would be ready to tell if they were on a *real* secret mission. More than that, there were too many unanswered questions. His soul wasn't going to let him rest till he had the answers and knew they were right.

Hogan gave the knife to Peterson and watched him work. Jakey got up from where he was sitting and started pacing back and forth behind the fire. He was back to acting like a good detective, about to question a prime suspect.

"But why was everybody looking for you?" he asked again. "Why didn't they know where you were?"

Sims shrugged. "Probably because nobody bothered to sit down and read our orders. Probably because the lieutenant in Houston thought we were supposed to be there on Saturday morning and, when we didn't show up, pushed the panic button."

"So why can't they find you? Why are you walking at night?"

Hogan even wanted to know the answer to that.

And it was a harder one to answer. "That's our fault," Sims confessed. "We had the orders a long time before we went to Houston. In fact, we kinda knew the new guy at Headquarters Division who made them out; he was with our division in Korea, so we knew what the orders were going to say, and we decided to put on a show."

Hogan didn't understand that, but Jakey did.

"We decided to show people what real Marines could do—"

"Like in *Battle Cry*," Jakey interrupted him. "That was a movie where this Marine battalion called Huxley's Harlots has to fight the top Marine brass to get a chance to hit the beaches first and show the world what it can do. When they finally got their beachhead it was someplace like Tarawa or Iwo Jima or Guadalcanal and half the battalion got wiped out."

"Something like that," Sims told him. "We just wanted to do something nobody else could do, walk four or five hundred miles, right through the middle of where people live, without anybody seeing us or even knowing we're there."

"Like a raid behind enemy lines," Jakey said. He couldn't think of a movie exactly like it; the Army went just as far in *Objective Burma* as to blow up an airfield, but it was through jungle and not where there were many Japanese; and there were a lot of movies about spies and guys escaping from the Germans, but they never had to go as far.

"Not quite," Sims corrected him. "If we were really behind enemy lines, you two would be the enemy, and you'd have turned us in when you first saw us, and we'd be shot. If this were a real war and you came up on us like this, we'd have cut your throats."

That was hard for Hogan to believe. "Even if we were just kids?" He'd never heard of anything like that, even in a movie. "Suppose you just tied us up?"

"No good. Only two things could happen: Either somebody would find you, in which case you'd turn us in, or you'd starve to death, which would be a horrible death. Cutting your throats," Sims told him, "would be the only humane thing to do."

Jakey knew Sims was right. If he were a marine, that's what he'd have to do, even if he didn't like it. The men and the mission would have to come first.

"But we're not behind enemy lines, and we're not going to cut your throats or tie you up." Hogan must have had a worried look on his face because Sims looked at him and added, "So don't worry."

But the situation did bring up a problem. Since they'd been seen, followed, and caught by Hogan and Jakey, what were they going to do?

Sims had been thinking about that but hadn't made up his mind. The only fair thing to do would be to walk into Sikes and turn themselves in to the local authorities, take credit for getting as far as they did, and take whatever else came.

Jakey and Hogan began to feel bad because they had ruined something they shouldn't have messed with. Jakey felt the worse because he was really the one who'd done it. He also thought the hardest to find some way to undo it.

And suddenly the answer was there, right in front

of his nose, and he was mad he hadn't seen it sooner.

"Okay," he said, "suppose we weren't the enemy, but on your side, like the people in the underground in France or the Filipinos in the islands or the Chinese. We'd be what you call partisans and we'd be on your side and help you out—"

"You could get us more beer!" Lofton said, clapping his hands with enthusiasm. If he knew he had some cold beer waiting for him in the morning, it sure would make walking all night a lot easier.

Jakey told them, "I got that, didn't I?" That was one of the things partisans did: get beer and food and things like Schnapps. To Jakey's mind it was a lot better to be known to the world as somebody who helped the marines get where they were going than the punk who turned them in.

"I'm not sure of all this," Hogan said. He had lost interest in the marines and gone back to dealing with his fish. Two of the fish were done, and the other one was cooking. "Tomorrow's Sunday and my father's got plans—"

In all his life Jakey had never had to deal with anybody so backward. "I'm only going to be here all summer. What's to keep him from doing it next week or any week for as many weeks as he wants to? I can get the beer and you can catch the fish."

Hogan still wasn't sure, so Jakey asked him what he'd do if there really were a war, be a Nazi or something, and that did it.

Before it got dark, they all made their plans. The marines had their briefing with the boys sitting in, and when it was over, Jones gave the briefing map to Jakey. Hogan set up camp, and when it got dark enough to move, the marines moved out.

18: Crossroads Church, 0300

One of the landmarks they watched for that night was a small community called Crossroads Church. From there they would look for an old logging road and follow it for about five miles; where it cut back into the state road west of Columbia, they would make camp for the day and wait for the boys.

They got to the community about ten minutes ahead of schedule, so Sims called a ten-minute break. Besides the old church, there were nine or ten houses clustered around the road, the houses unpainted for years, the siding planks weathered and twisted, the windows dark and unfriendly. A single streetlight in front of a general store lit the area. The trees in the graveyard behind the church were hung with moss and made the graveyard look the way graveyards ought to look, frightening enough to make living people want to keep living. Sims used the light to write in his journal during the rest break and wrote:

> There was a battle fought here, I can feel it. It wasn't a big or famous battle, or I'd have read about it. It was one of those kinds of fights that happened on the move, here at this crossroad one day, twenty miles away the next. If it wasn't in the Civil War, then it was in the French and Indian, or War of 1812, or some war between Indians that had no name. People were always fighting.
>
> The more I think about it, the sadder it makes me feel. There's really no such thing as PEACE. When kids can't wait to grow up and either get in a war or start one of their own, then peace is nothing more than a waiting period between generations. That's what this country is doing right now, waiting for the kids to get old enough to die.

Sims began to think that in a way what he was doing by letting those two kids get beer for the squad was letting them practice for their war. In a way he was doing something even worse: He was helping make sure that they'd want to have one. Hell, they were ready to join right now; they didn't even have to do any more growing.

Well, he was going to put a stop to that. They had had their little game, and when they showed up again that afternoon, that was going to be the end of it.

19: Ahead of the Game

It took almost all day to do everything they had to do, but Jakey and Hogan got it all done. In the morning they'd ridden back to Sikes, where Hogan found a drugstore open and called home. It was during church, but rather than wait around the drugstore for an hour making the druggist suspicious, Hogan called anyway and let the phone ring till the Kavanaughs, who lived down the road and shared their party line, got tired of hearing it and answered the phone. The message he gave them was that he and Jakey were fine and were having a lot of fun and were going to have to stay gone a little longer; he would explain it when he got home. The Kavanaughs said they would deliver the message.

While Hogan was on the phone, Jakey was looking at the telephone book and discovering something interesting, something that reminded him of a trick he'd seen pulled in Memphis. All the doctors in that part of the country who had offices in different towns—Sikes, Columbia, Grayson, Vixen, Olla— were listed in the Yellow Pages of the same book. There were three doctors listed for Columbia: Drs. Riorson, Johnson, and Pierce. Like the con man he was, Jakey told the druggist a story about meeting a boy in camp whose father was a doctor in Columbia and not being able to remember his name.

The druggist, of course, knew all the doctors, and their wives and families, and all the vets and dentists, too. "You must be thinking of Dr. Walter Johnson," he said. "He's got a boy your age."

What Jakey knew was that sometimes opportunities presented themselves to you—like the beer truck—but most of the time you had to make them yourself.

The druggist in Sikes gave him a piece of scratch paper from his note pad when he asked for it, with the name of his pharmacy printed on the top. It never did hurt to advertise.

He and Hogan had spent the night in the tent, eaten one of *their* sorry meals for breakfast, and doubled back through Sikes to make the phone call and get on Road Number 126 to Grayson. From Grayson, which was twenty-three miles away, they had to ride another three miles north to Columbia, then back east for about a mile till they hit the tracks. The bicycle baskets were considerably lighter since everything had been eaten—steaks, the girls' prize vegetables, even the ice in the cooler.

It was a good four-hour ride to Grayson mainly because of the hills and the fact that they were still in timber country, where pulpwood was loaded on the trucks that flew down the road. Every time they heard one coming, the best thing to do was to get over on the shoulder and let it go by.

In downtown Grayson, which wasn't anything to

brag on unless you liked filling stations, hardware stores, and truck stops, they stopped and ate a greasy cheeseburger apiece on Jakey's money and split a malted milk. Then they rode on to Columbia on Highway 165, rather on the side of Highway 165, to keep from getting flattened out like turtles.

Columbia was a little bit bigger, but not so big that they could get lost, and they didn't have any trouble finding either the road they were looking for or the kind of store that Jakey was looking for.

On the piece of notepad paper, Jakey hadn't written an address, only the instructions "Please let the two boys get the beer and picnic supplies I need. I'll be by to pay you for them later, so it is the same as selling it to me." The note signed "Dr. Walter Johnson."

They carried everything up to the counter, and the clerk looked at them, and at the beer, and shook his head no. Jakey handed him the note, and the man not only let them take it all but helped load it in the cooler and basket and threw in a bag of ice free.

"The way to get what you want," Jakey bragged, seeing that Hogan was impressed, "is to get a doctor to say it's all right." That was the trick he'd learned in Memphis.

If the marines were where they were supposed to be, this was going to be a good party.

20: War Stories

The original question that started it all was completely innocent. Lofton had sat down by Peterson and opened a can of beer and swallowed about half of it in one gulp. "You ever tasted anything so good?" he'd asked, more to make a comment than ask a real question.

Peterson, though, took the question seriously and tried to think of something that had tasted better. "Once I got run over by a truck," he said, and Hogan and Jakey could tell from the look on his face that he was telling the truth. There were a lot of cans being popped open and a lot of oohing and ahing, but Peterson had the floor.

"I was on KP at Quantico, and they had me on garbage detail. We had to empty all the garbage cans and put 'em upside down over this steam nozzle . . . steam will clean anything. It was out back of the chow hall where we were working, and that day they'd served green pea soup, which nobody ever would eat—it was worse than liver. Out comes this big fifty-five-gallon can full of green pea soup that's turned so cold it's like concrete. The guys I worked with knew I was strong, and they made a bet with the cooks that I couldn't pick it up. So I picked it up, bear-hugged it; but it weighed so much it made my legs wobble, and I wobbled out in front of a truck. When I woke up, I had that soup everywhere—in my nose, in my ears and hair. I thought I was going to suffocate in it, but I was alive. I swallowed a big mouthful so I could breathe, and somebody poured some water down my throat. They say the truck hit the can of soup first, and that saved me. All I know is that water was the best thing I ever tasted in my life."

Sims had taken the guard so they could all have an even six beers each. Six cans of beer would be good for them, he figured, since they'd just walked more than twenty miles and in three hours were going to walk over twenty more. All he'd asked them was to watch their language and not cuss around the kids.

"I'd rather drink water right out of the swamp than that stuff that runs through the pipes at Quantico," Lofton said, settling back against a log and closing his eyes. "Nothing is as bad as the water at Quantico."

That got Jones going—Jones, who this night didn't have to study maps. "I tasted water a lot worse than Quantico," he said, also relaxing. "Once in Korea we made camp where there was this well. The medics checked out the water; the cooks cooked with it; everything was supposed to be all right. Only to me it tasted bad, and I didn't drink it but once.

"We were there a couple of days . . . I can't remember how many . . . and one day we look down in the well, and there's this dead goat floating in it. The Chinese had tried to weight him down with our old artillery casings."

Ross took exception to that. "Artillery casings," he

stated. "Those things were solid brass, and I almost made a fortune selling them in Seoul." He swore he would have, too, if they hadn't signed the armistice and ended the war.

"Police action," Russell corrected him. You could lose a stripe for calling the thing a war because wars were things that were officially declared and officially won or lost. The brass didn't want to ruin a perfect record.

They argued among themselves then, over what it was, a war or a police action. It was almost as though the two kids weren't there, and Groh, the medic, finally ended the argument by asking what difference it made.

"You got a stomach wound, you gonna yell 'war' or 'police action' or 'medic.'" Groh had treated more stomach wounds than most doctors would in a lifetime. "Tell them about Sims," he said, looking at Hopper. Hopper and Sims had gone through Korea together, and Sims would never talk about what had happened.

"Nobody told us about the Chinese." Hopper started talking, and everybody knew right away the mood had changed. There was a vacant look on his face, and it was probably caused by everything—the beer, the walking, and the stories the others had told. "Our company was on the line, just below the Yalu River, and they came across. That night was the first night they blew the bugles, and you never heard anything till you heard those bugles, and they charged our guns till they couldn't walk for all the bodies.

"The next night it was the same thing, and we were all on the line again. Both nights Sims was on the fifty-caliber machine gun.

"The third night he was back on it again, not in the same place, of course, because we were in the big retreat, fighting day and night, trying to make it down to Hungnam, where they were going to ship us out, a hundred-and-ten-mile retreat. It was the third night, like I say, and he was sitting there numb—he'd killed so many people—just sitting there, watching one of their trucks burning on the side of a hill across the way. What he was looking at was the way it seemed to go out every once in a while, and he thought that was odd, how a fire that big could go out and come back on again. Then he figured it out: Somebody was walking between him and the truck, and he cut loose with that machine gun.

"They sent up flares, and there they were, the whole Chinese Army coming at us. The third night they hadn't blown the bugles.

"We made it to Hungnam," Hopper concluded. "and when they finally got around to it, they gave Sims a medal. In just three nights he'd not only saved our whole company but killed more Chinese than probably anybody in the whole war."

And it was a *war*, Hopper said, no matter what the brass called it.

That night the kids ate Marine chow. Lofton heated the water, which tasted bad from the purification tablets, and mixed it with powdered macaroni and cheese, soup—not green pea, thank goodness—and powdered milk. The squad had gone through the canned ham quicker than they'd gone through the beer.

When it started to get dark, Sims came off watch and called the briefing together. It was a short one since all they were going to do that night was walk the tracks north and east to a town called Bosco, then cut due east to pick up a dirt road through the cotton fields. The next meeting with the kids was set for a stand of trees southeast of the junction of State Roads 132 and 622 near the town of Mangham.

21: Columbia, 2110

By Sims's calculations, the boys had been gone from their home three nights: the night by the railroad junction below Winnfield, the night by Flatt Creek, and this night, east of Columbia. Mangham was going to be four, and four nights were too many for parents not to start worrying and calling the police. Two boys on their bicycles riding around in broad daylight—how could someone not have seen them?

He didn't like what he was about to do, and the men wouldn't like it either; but he had to do something to start a false trail, and he had to do it now. They were getting too close to the end of the trip to get caught now.

The first part of what he had told the kids was right; when they left the camp that night, they headed east to the railroad tracks and then north on the tracks toward Bosco. They got above Columbia and came to a narrow pass where the tracks cut through the steep walls of a clay hill, a protected place where they could risk a light, and Sims stopped them.

"Let me have the maps," he said, and Jones gave them to him. He studied them for a few minutes, squatting on his haunches between the rails with the rest of the men looking on. "Okay," he finally said, "here it is . . . change of plans." In a mile they would leave the tracks and take a road east. They would cross the Ouachita, and they'd keep going east till they hit the town of Hebert. They would cut around town on the west side and head north and east again till they hit a farm road that paralleled the Boeuf River, cross at a low water bridge, and start following Big Piney Creek. They'd stop at the creek when they were west of Winnsboro and make camp for the day.

For a minute or two the men in the squad were quiet, thinking about what the new route really meant. The boys were going to Mangham, a good fifteen miles to the north and west.

"So we're just gonna dump them," Lofton said. Lofton had sort of liked having the boys around, and the idea of getting a cold beer and something real to eat hadn't bothered him too much either.

"They'll be all right," Sims assured them. "They'll get up to Mangham and look around for us, and when we don't show up, they'll go home. You guys know where we're going and you know what we've got to cross."

What Sims was talking about was the Mississippi River, something the men in the squad hadn't thought about for a while.

"How would you feel if we let them keep going and they got hurt or killed?" That was argument enough to convince them that he was right.

"We wouldn't really have done it, would we?" That was Peterson, and nobody in the squad ever quite knew what Peterson was thinking about most of the time. "We wouldn't really have cut their throats?" This time he was remembering what Sims had said earlier about wartime and being discovered behind enemy lines.

Sims started to say something about how nobody knew what he was going to do in a situation till he got in it, but that wasn't what Peterson wanted to hear. "Of course not," Sims said, and that was all he was going to say.

22: Red, White, Blue, and Banana Cream

It was July 2, a Monday, and all across Louisiana farmers and their families were on their way to town. Back in Natchitoches the McGhees, except for Grandma McGhee, had come in to buy their monthly supplies and do their other business: banking; looking at clothes; seeing things that they couldn't see on the farm, even in catalogues. Grandma McGhee loved to go to town more than anything, but because the boys weren't at home yet and might call again, she had been elected to stay at home. Gilbert himself had decided to give the boys until that afternoon to get their hides home, and he hoped they had a good excuse for missing church. If they weren't back, he was going to send Pigiron out to get them. The girls all thought that Hogan ought to get a whipping; not Jakey, though, because it wasn't his fault.

Hogan and Jakey not only were not back at the farm that afternoon, but were still headed in the opposite direction, and the afternoon found them in the town of Mangham. It hadn't been an easy ride for them because of all the traffic. There were more people in Mangham than there were in Natchitoches that day, and there was a reason for it.

When you're a hundred years old, you're allowed to celebrate, and that's what the town of Mangham was doing. It had been incorporated for a century, and its people were proud of it. A banner stretched between the first two downtown light poles coming into town said "THE GOOD OLD DAYS ARE HERE AGAIN IN MANGHAM," and just about everything that could be wrapped with red, white, and blue crepe paper was: the light poles; buildings; houses; even trees and cars.

The two boys came riding their bikes into town like Roman conquerors back from a trip up the Nile, or at least that's the way Jakey was thinking of it. Hogan thought it was embarrassing, since there suddenly wasn't any other traffic on the street, and people were looking at them.

Ahead of them was a three-block section that was closed off to cars; that explained why everybody around them was walking. The boys rode up to the barricade and got off their bikes. "Let's split up and scout around," Jakey suggested, and Hogan was all for it. He turned around to agree, but Jakey was already back on his bike and riding off down a side street.

Mangham was not much different from the other towns they'd been through—the same kind of downtown and the same kind of people in it—but it seemed more interesting because everything was so decorated and so many people were dressed up. Just about everybody was wearing old-timey clothes, and the men who didn't have real sideburns, mustaches, and beards had fake ones—some of them so fake they'd been drawn on with grease pencils.

Hogan looked around for a safe place to leave his

bike and equipment and in the first block found a bar-
bershop, where the barber let him bring it in and lean
it against the wall.

"Better let me stick some hair on your chin," the
barber said, offering him a ball of somebody's hair
that he'd collected in a paper sack. "Anybody who
don't have hair on their face gets thrown in jail."
Hogan thanked him but no; he'd take his chances.

Back on the street and down a block there was a
crowd of people who were even more dressed up than
everybody else. They were mingling around in front
of a big wooden stage that took up half the street. The
men looked like riverboat gamblers, and the women
like dance hall girls, except you could tell they
weren't real floozies. Everybody on the stage, and
there were about ten of them, was trying to look his-
torical, and one of the men actually did look a little
bit like Abraham Lincoln. But three of the people
onstage were different. There was a skinny, rawboned
man with a cowboy string tie and a huge silver eagle
belt buckle, and he was holding a yellow fiddle. There
was a woman with long blond hair who was wearing
fancy blue jeans and purple boots, holding a guitar.
And there was another man who was wearing regular
farmer's coveralls, almost hiding behind a big accor-
dion that sparkled in the sunlight like diamonds.
They came up to the front of the stage and started
playing a song that started out as a Cajun song but
then began to change, and the woman started giving

square dance calls for the crowd that was mingling, and they started square dancing.

Hogan didn't care much for any kind of dancing, square or otherwise, and so walked on. In that second block all the store windows featured old-fashioned clothes and hardware and appliances, like butter churns and wringer washers and iceboxes that took real ice instead of electricity. There were price tags on them, so people could see what they cost when they were new, and there were pictures of people buying them and taking them home in the days when the streets were still dirt and people came to town in wagons.

In the next block there was an American Legion post with its windows decorated to show off the town's war history, with pictures of the local National Guard unit that went to fight in France and big pictures of the officers and the people who got medals. There was also a plaque that listed the names of everybody who got killed.

If there ever came another war, Hogan had made up his mind to join the Air Force; it seemed the best way to keep his name off just such a list. He knew what Jakey would do: join the Marines. The trouble with Jakey was he'd probably talk Hogan into joining the Marines with him and volunteering for the front lines. In a way everything was more fun with Jakey around, and the summer had already turned out to be a success; but it wouldn't break his heart if Jakey decided to go back and keep living in Memphis. Hogan could already imagine what Jakey would be like in school.

The last thing in that third block, on the edge of town, really, was a building that stood alone and apart from the others and had a modern, familiar shape. It was a Dairy Freeze and hadn't been in business very long, yet it took part in the celebration, too, with a sign on the window that said, "Our prices haven't gone up!" Cones were a dime when they opened in 1950 and they were still a dime, milk shakes were a quarter and were still a quarter, and Hogan just happened to have a quarter that he wasn't using.

On his way back up the street, he heard the music end and something else start. Somebody had a microphone and was asking all the people who'd signed up as contestants to come to the stage because the contest was about to start. When he got there, he could see from a big sign that it was going to be a pie-eating contest, and that was something he wanted to see, so he worked his way through the crowd to get front, right there on the innermost ring. The first thing he noticed was that instead of men contestants, it was going to be kids, and then he saw that one of the kids sitting at a long contestant table was Jakey.

In front of the table there was a man with an official-looking movie camera set up on tripod, and Hogan suspected that explained everything. Jakey wasn't going to miss a chance to get in a movie.

There were five contestants in all, Jakey and four

boys who weren't necessarily taller but who out-weighed him so much that they made him look absolutely skinny. There wasn't any way to describe them except fat.

A pie-eating contest against those four boys was going to be too pitiful to watch.

But Jakey saw him and smiled and waved, and there wasn't anything Hogan could do but watch.

All five of them were sitting at the table facing the crowd, and facing them, lined up on the table in even rows, were four slightly large pies. On a separate table off to the side, there was another four pies waiting, in case they were needed.

"The order of the contest," the announcer explained, "is lemon meringue, apple, chocolate, and banana cream. All of one pie must be eaten entirely, filling, topping, and crust, before another pie can be started." He looked at his notes and read the names of the women in the community who had baked and contributed the pies and how nothing had been scrimped in their making. "Mrs. Juanita Mills, who made the banana creams," he said, as an example, "tells me that she put six whole bananas in each one of her pies, and I read somewhere that the world's record for eating bananas was only ten."

He then wanted especially to thank Dr. Raymond Crandell of the Crandell Clinic for standing by with a stomach pump in case there were any medical emergencies. "Show it to them, Doc," he said, and the doctor opened his case and took out the pump for the boys to see. It was an ugly, nasty-looking thing with the part that fitted over your face looking like a gas mask and the part that slid down your throat looking like a giant, black, slimy eel. The slimy eel part jiggled around like it was alive and gave a person goosebumps to think about its sliding down a throat.

It didn't seem to faze the four fat boys, though, three of whom were already dipping their fingers in the first pie to warm up.

Then the announcer asked them all if they were ready and said, "Okay . . . go!" and they went. It was clear that Jakey had never been in a pie-eating contest before because he didn't have the proper manners. He began by cutting his first pie into neat pieces and starting on the first piece. The four fat boys dug in and crammed handfuls into lower jaws that sprung open and closed like cash registers. Jakey ate steadily and neatly, picking up each piece with his knife and not biting off more than he could chew. When he got a little meringue on his chin, he wiped it off with his napkin and smiled at the movie camera before he took another bite, hamming it up for all it was worth. The fat boys were covered from their noses halfway down their necks with pie. They were starting on their third pies, the chocolates, before Jakey finished the first; they had slowed down considerably, though, and Jakey was still going steadily.

By the time the fat boys were on that third pie their

faces had strained looks on them, and they were making infrequent digs into the chocolate muck they'd created. They looked a little bit as if they'd been tarred and feathered, and the crowd was loving it, some of the people laughing so hard that they could barely stand up.

The first fat boy dropped out on a run when the doctor took out the stomach pump again and wiggled it in front of them. This time, instead of looking worried, Jakey smiled and waved again and stood up for a stretch and a few stomach exercises with his arms over his head. He had finished the second pie, the apple, and was licking his lips at the third, the chocolate. Probably nothing could have discouraged the remaining fat boy more than his cutting the third pie into neat pieces, smiling, and asking for a new napkin. By that time the camera was on him almost exclusively and turned back to the others only for comedy relief.

Two of the three fat boys who were left finished the chocolate and started on the banana cream, the killer, but the third one just continued to study what was left of his chocolate pie, while Jakey, slowly and steadily taking bite after bite, passed him. If Jakey was getting full or even getting close to filling up, you couldn't tell it by his expression.

Of the two boys eating on the bananas, one had barely begun, and you just knew he wasn't going to take another bite, even with his parents and relatives down front cheering him on. The other one was about halfway through his yellow glop but digging at it with only two fingers at a time.

By that time there wasn't a person in the crowd who didn't know that Jakey was going to win. He got up, stretched, and waved to the crowd and did some more stomach exercises. That gave the only remaining contender the same idea, and he got up and stretched. He wasn't going to be outhammed either, and instead of waving, he pulled up the bottom of his T-shirt and showed the crowd his enormous belly. Then he sat back down and grabbed up a big handful; he bravely shoved it in his mouth, using his fingers to get it in and keep it in, but he couldn't swallow it, and he had to cup his hands over his mouth to catch it as it came tumbling out. That did it for the other boy, too, who broke the flimsy chair he was sitting in in his haste to get away from that banana cream pie.

That left only Jakey. The judge looked at how much they'd all eaten and ruled that Jakey had to eat two more pieces before he would be the winner. Calm as a duck in a zoo, with flashbulbs popping left and right, he ate the last pieces and part of a third.

They interviewed him for the papers and took more pictures of him with his prizes. One of his prizes was a .22 bolt-action rifle, worth only fifteen dollars and good only for squirrels and rabbits, but important because it was Jakey's first gun. The other prize was a banana cream pie.

23: Among the Squirrels and Cotton

It was hard to ride the bike over bumps without messing up the pie; but the pie was in a box, thank goodness, and Jakey was doing his best. It was tied to the top of his backpack and equipment in the basket, so it wasn't in any danger of falling or getting bumped out. The only trouble was, the top of the box was starting to turn a different color, and that was a bad sign.

The rifle was slung across his back with a piece of rope the way a true partisan's rifle ought to be carried. In his pocket he carried a box of fifty .22 long bullets, and he couldn't wait to get out of town, find the marines, and show it to them. He was going to see what they thought about him and Hogan changing their roles from partisans to scouts. A scout was about the same thing, except he had more responsibilities, like going out and hunting and bringing back fresh meat.

"That's the silliest crap I ever heard of," Hogan told him after listening to his plan. "You know how long you'd have to hunt to get ten or twenty squirrels with a single-shot twenty-two? You'd be hunting all day and all night; then you'd have to skin 'em out and cook 'em. Can you even call a squirrel?"

Jakey had seen squirrels before; there were at least a dozen living in the oaks behind his house in Memphis and thousands of them in the park. "Squirrels don't need calling," he argued, and that made Hogan laugh.

"There's a big difference," he tried to explain, "between the tame kind that live in town and the wild ones that live out here. In town they eat out of your hand, and out here they'll *eat* your hand. There's not one within a mile of us that doesn't know we're here, and they're faster than homemade lightning." Hogan had another thought as well. "The marines don't want attention, but if you go to shooting that rifle, that's just what we'll get. This isn't hunting season, and this isn't our land."

Jakey turned sharply to avoid a two-foot-wide hole in the thin crust of the road and stopped his bike. They had come to the intersection of country roads south and east of the town where they were supposed to meet the squad. "Shooting can wait till we're back home," he decided.

In the back of the shallow field ahead of them were the woods where they were supposed to make contact. There was cotton growing in the field, as the land outside Columbia had flattened out and gotten more farmable. Pushing the bikes down one of the rows to get to the woods was no problem; it hadn't rained in quite a while, and the fields were good and dry. The only problem was the smell of crop dust in the field, which Hogan estimated couldn't be more than a day old. If you got some rotten eggs and cooked them in a skillet, that's what crop dust would smell like.

"Louisiana," Jakey felt compelled to say, "has more bad smells than any state in the Union."

At any other time in any other situation those would've been fighting words, but this time Hogan let them pass. "You like wearing shirts and pants," he said matter-of-factly, "so don't complain about where they come from."

When they were out of sight of the road, they leaned their bikes against trees and started looking around.

"Let me see that map again," Jakey said, holding out his hand. He didn't feel too good from eating all that pie, and he was getting tired of tramping around the woods as they were doing, getting farther and farther away from the bicycles. He looked at the road maps they'd brought with them, and two things were certain: They were in the right place—where the marines had said they'd be—and the marines weren't there.

The sunlight was fading, and they didn't have much more than an hour of it left. If they were going to make a decision, it had to be now.

"Okay," Jakey said, "we're here, and they're not. Something might have happened to hold them up, or they might not have made as many miles as they thought they would." Hogan had thought of both those possibilities. "So the thing for us to do is go ahead and pitch camp in the right place and wait for them to show up tonight," Jakey figured.

"On one condition," Hogan said. "I don't care whether they ever show up or not; in the morning we head back home." You know a trip is about over when you start looking forward to your own bed, and Hogan was doing more than that. Since they'd parked their bikes, that's all he'd been able to think about.

Some of the air in Jakey's sails had leaked out with the marines' not being there, that and the feeling he had in his legs, which was like his body weighed 1,000 pounds. But he wasn't ready yet to call it quits. Everything could change in the next two hours, and that was a fact. "Let's go set up and see what happens," he said, carefully not agreeing or going against any conditions.

24: On the Pipeline, 0030

While the boys settled into camp in the woods near Mangham, Sims and the squad had crawled out of their bags in a pine forest north of Winnsboro and were on their way again northeast. What was done with the kids was done, and most of the men accepted it and put it out of their minds. The only one who hadn't completely let it go was Ross because Ross never let anything go till he worked out all the details. He had put it out of his mind for the moment, though, because like the rest of the squad, he could see what was coming and see that it was a bigger problem.

For the last five miles they had been following an underground pipeline. It had to be one that was still in service because the company that owned it kept the ground on top cleared of trees and brush, and that made for some easy and protected walking. Ahead of them, though, the pipe, maybe four feet in diameter, suddenly rose from the ground in a sharp angle and climbed to a height of fifteen feet.

Three-Finger Hopper looked at the pipe and gave Jones a nervous laugh. "I think you find these things on purpose," he said. "You take us out of our way to find these things."

The reason he was nervous was the reason the pipe started running aboveground: a mile-wide depression in the earth where Deer Creek became Deer Creek Lake, as black and foul a body of water as any in the world.

"If I fall off that damned thing," Groh wanted them all to know, "don't start getting cute. Get me out of there fast." The rest of the squad murmured in agreement.

They all took off their boots and socks and stuffed them in their packs. Because Lofton could climb the best, Sims gave him a rope and sent him up first.

Three-Finger Hopper was next up, with Lofton haul-
ing on the rope and hugging him at the top to keep
him steady. "First breather you get, why don't you
wash your putrid body?" Lofton suggested. "You
stink worse than something dead."

Since they hadn't really washed themselves since
the cattle watering tank at the McGhee farm, they all
smelled like swamp rot. "May I suggest the same for
you?" Hopper said, turning to breathe the rarefied air
above the ground. Then they pulled up the others together, Lofton kept the rope handy, and they started
walking.

There wasn't a house within miles of them, and nobody was likely to be out on that black water at night.
The moon was up, but it was full and high in the sky.
Their shadows were almost directly under their feet,
so they wouldn't look like Halloween cats on a fence.
They couldn't even see the water under them, but
they didn't have to in order to know it was there.
Things—fish, snakes, or turtles—were constantly
making some kind of noise, and the noise reminded
Hopper of one of his worst nightmares, one in which
he had fallen into a nest of snakes, and when his
friends pulled him out, he had skinny green snakes
with black heads hanging all over his body, and he
was dead.

It was good practice for Vicksburg, where the bridge
would be higher, where their time over water would

be longer, and there was no question of your being dead if you fell. The bridge was worrying Sims a lot more than this easy pipe.

They hadn't been on the pipe for more than a few minutes when strange things began to happen to them. Russell felt it first, a kind of weightless vertigo that a person might get from walking on a trampoline. Groh was next; only to him it felt like he'd lost control over his legs. Peterson thought he was getting dizzy from being so far out on the lake. Sims's first thought was that they were getting oil fumes from the pipe, in which case they were in bad trouble and might be better off taking to the water.

One by one they first crouched, then sat down on the pipe to keep their balance. Everything had gone into a state of confusion. In place of the noises that had been coming from the lake below them there now came an intense silence. It was as if the lake had ceased to exist and they were on a tightrope in space, except space itself wasn't even there. Then it was all over.

It had been a vibration, one that had come on so fast that it affected the muscles in their legs and disturbed their sense of balance. Sitting on the pipe, they could feel the vibration change, slow down enough for them to know what it was and what was causing it. Oil was flowing through the pipe for the first time since they'd been over it or on it. It must have come pushing through under pressure like a torpedo coming out a tube.

The vibrations continued slowing till they became a steady sway, and the lake and its noises came back.

"Let's get off this thing," Sims suggested, and in four more minutes of fast walking they were over. It hadn't been as easy as it had looked; but it was behind them now, and they climbed down and put on their socks and boots.

They had planned to rest and eat on the other side of the lake, but the shaking they'd been through had taken away their appetites, so they just rested for a few minutes. There were still eight more miles of pipe to follow before they changed directions and headed east again.

Ross had gone back to puzzling about the kids, and it suddenly occurred to him what was wrong. He was a slow-talking man from Georgia who had a good mind but had a hard time expressing himself. The Marines might have made him an officer if he hadn't had such a long, bony face and talked so much like a hick. He came and sat down by Sims and said, "I've been doing some thinking." Sims waited patiently for him to go on. "I've been thinking about those two kids, and I think that we maybe made a big mistake." This time Sims didn't wait but told him to spit it out. "Now didn't we tell them that we were on our way to march in a Fourth of July parade?"

Sims remembered back to the first time he'd talked to the kids and the one called Jakey had given him the third degree. "I told them we were on our way to raise a flag in a cemetery and march in a parade. I could have said Fourth of July."

"I think you did," Ross said. "So when you stop and think about it, how hard would it be for them two kids to figure out that we're heading to Vicksburg?"

Sims had to admit that it wouldn't be too hard.

"Well, what would you do if you were a kid? Would you go home, or would you keep going on your own to Vicksburg? Kids like them two will do anything, especially that one called Jakey."

"We can't be responsible for what they do or don't do," Sims said, not knowing what they could do about it if they were.

"Seems like we can't," Ross said, meaning more than he was saying, "but if one of them gets killed on that bridge over there, we're gonna get asked an awful lot of questions, and we might start thinking about some of the answers. They're gonna try that bridge," Ross said, getting up and climbing back into his pack, "unless somebody's there to stop them."

"Damn it, Ross," Sims said, "why didn't you tell me this yesterday?"

All Ross could do was shrug. "I guess because I didn't think about it yesterday."

They might not be able to stop them—the kids

were on bicycles, and they were not—but the only thing they could do was try. Sims cut the rest period short and, when the squad was ready, ordered double time.

25: On to Vicksburg

Three times during the night Jakey had awakened and crawled out of the tent to look around for the marines, and all three times he'd drawn a blank. By the time he got to sleeping his best sleep it was morning and he had to get up. Hogan had pulled the tent pegs out of the ground and let the thing almost smother him. When he came crawling out, Hogan was dressed and leaning against the side of a tree with his hands in his pocket, looking at him. The look on his face was one of pure disgust.

"Well, what's wrong with you?" Jakey asked him, yawning and pulling on his socks.

"You wake me up three times to get up and look around; then when you finally go to sleep, you start stinking so bad you chase me out of the tent."

Jakey smelled his armpits for Hogan's benefit and wrinkled his nose. "Don't see how I smell any worse than you. How do you know it wasn't yourself you were smelling?"

Hogan threw his sleeping bag in the bike basket. "Because I didn't eat four pies and pass their gas all night," he said, and Jakey just smiled. He pulled Jakey's sleeping bag out of the tent and started folding the tent. "I figure we're about seventy miles from home. If we take good roads and ride like hell, we might get there by midnight."

Jakey pulled on his jeans and slipped his feet in the tennis shoes, but he made no move toward pulling on his shirt. Instead, he got out their Louisiana road maps and stretched out on his stomach on the sleeping bag. After a few minutes he said, "I think I know where they are," and Hogan threw up his hands and groaned.

He started counting the things against them on his fingers: "We're out of money. We're out of food. We stink to high heaven. We're seventy miles away from home, and we've been lucky 'cause it hasn't rained. My father's going to be mad, and we're probably both gonna get big whippings. We're already two days late, and by the time we get back we'll be three. We've missed church, and I've missed doing all my chores. We've eaten almost all of my sisters' prize canned goods, and *you* have stolen stuff and forged a doctor's name—"

"You can have the rifle," Jakey said, not even looking up, as if giving Hogan his rifle would make it all right. As for getting a whipping . . . "I've been whipped by experts," he said.

Hogan loaded the tent and looked at his cousin, who was yet to make a motion toward leaving. "I'll give you five minutes," Hogan said. "If you're not ready to go in five minutes, I'm going without you."

Giving Jakey Darby five minutes was a mistake. He swung around to sit cross-legged and cleared a place in the dirt in front of him.

"Okay," he said, "here we are in Mangham." He made scratches in the dirt, and Hogan came over to listen to his bunk. "Here we were night before last, and here we were the night before that."

"And *this* is where we've got to be by tonight," Hogan said, making a mark for the farm with his own stick.

Jakey just ignored him and went on. "Now this is the Mississippi River, and here's Vicksburg. Ever since we've been following them and ever since they left Houston, they've been heading straight toward Vicksburg when there's probably been a lot easier ways to walk. So what's the reason?"

"Because that's the way they're going," Hogan answered, almost in desperation. "When you're walking somewhere, you walk there. What's so hard to figure out?"

"I'll tell you what," Jakey said, getting a little exasperated himself. "If you were going to swim, you could swim anywhere; and if you'd hidden out boats to get across, you could get the boats and cross any-where. But if you were going to cross on a bridge, you'd have to go where there was a bridge, and there's only one bridge from here"—he pointed to Natchez—"and here"—he pointed to Greenville. "There's no-place else where the road crosses the river."

Hogan sat down on the ground beside Jakey and started pleading with him. "My father's worried and probably out looking for us in the ranger district. He probably thinks we've drowned or been kidnapped."

"And my father's dead," Jakey said, now starting to get mad. "So nobody cares what I do and what I don't do. Go home and get your whipping if that's what you want." Jakey pulled on his shirt and slung the rifle across his back. "I'm going to Vicksburg."

If Hogan had any choices, he didn't know what they were. He couldn't leave Jakey on his own, and if he called home, what would he say?

"You can go back if you want to," Jakey said, "but remember that you promised not to say anything about the marines, and if you tell them where I am, that would be the same thing." From the look on Hogan's face, Jakey knew he had him. "I say we both go on, and when it's all over, call your father to come get us or send us the money for a bus. When we tell him what we've done, he won't be mad."

Hogan was stuck, just plain stuck, but he wasn't giving in without one more try. "What do we get for all this?" he asked. "Tell me, what is it we're supposed to get?"

"We get to say we did it. We get to say we went with the missing marines when nobody else could find them, not even the FBI, halfway across the state of Louisiana. We could even get to be famous."

"I'm not going to say you talked me into it," Hogan said, getting on his bike and walking it around till it was pointed in the right direction. "I can just see that I'm not going to talk you out, so whatever happens happens to us both."

Between both of them they had enough change in their pockets to buy three cans of soup, with Hogan holding back a dime to make a phone call if he had to. It was ten in the morning when they rode back through Mangham to get on 132 to Tallulah. It was Tuesday, July 3.

26: Tallulah

As concerned Tuesday, July 3, weathermen would say, officially, what everybody in Louisiana knew: that it was the hottest day of the year so far and getting hotter. By noon that day the temperature had climbed to 95, and by two in the afternoon, with Jakey and Hogan riding their bikes into the outskirts of Tallulah, it hit 100. Hogan was riding in front again, with Jakey struggling along behind him, the heat boiling up from the road so thick that it looked like water. "Right now at my house," he called back, "my mother is probably getting everybody into the kitchen for ice cream." The thought of a malted milk and a double scoop of ice cream floating in it was all that was keeping Jakey going.

Hogan, unfortunately, was wrong about what was going on at that moment at home. His mother was there all right, waiting for a phone call from him or Jakey. The rest of the family was in the old church bus, though, and was hot on the boys' trail. True to his word, Gilbert McGhee had come back from town on Monday afternoon and sent Pigiron and the dog Benny out to find them; when nobody came back and the rangers over there hadn't seen them, he decided to do some investigating on his own. That morning he'd called the telephone company and had it trace Hogan's call back to the drugstore in Sikes. When he announced that he was going to Sikes to look for them, Grandma McGhee announced that she was going, too, and then the girls wanted to go, and that meant taking lunches and the church bus.

In Sikes they saw Pigiron and Benny walking, still following the boys' trail, this time around the sidewalks in town. They picked them up, and Pigiron told them the details of how Benny had sniffed out another trail, one that belonged to eight to ten soldiers. And either the boys were following the soldiers or the soldiers were following them. It didn't make a whole lot of sense because the boys were on bicycles and the soldiers were on foot, and it looked like they were making camp in the same place at different times, the soldiers during the day and the boys at night.

In Sikes Gilbert McGhee decided to contact the local parish sheriff, and from the sheriff he found out about the missing case of beer and talked to the driver of the truck, who identified Hogan's picture. That made it even more of a puzzle because Hogan was too much of an athlete to start drinking beer. He even planned to go out for football in the fall.

When he found out about the question Jakey had asked the druggist about Dr. Johnson in Columbia, he had to admit he was stumped.

So it was that at the moment when Hogan thought the family was sitting down to a dish of ice cream, they were actually on their way to Columbia, Louisiana, where they would be even more confused.

"It keeps getting hotter," Jakey moaned, knowing he had to stop soon and cool off, or else he was going to die. He was seeing flashing black jagged circles around the edges of his vision.

"I think that's Tallulah," Hogan told him. If it were, there would be a bayou running from one end of town to the other, a bayou that a person could safely jump in without jumping into a nest of snakes.

The bayou was there. It was Tallulah, and their riding work was almost done. They were only fifteen flat, easy pumping miles from the bridge.

After they had had their swim, fully clothed except for shoes, they took off their T-shirts and hung them on branches in the sun. In about five minutes their shirts were dry, and though the shirts smelled kind of like dead fish, they weren't as bad-smelling as they had been before. Hogan sat looking at the bayou for a while, thinking that there had to be fish in it at some time or another and wondering if there still were. Water close to town like this had a way of getting fished out pretty fast. Hot as it was, though, no fish would be biting. They'd be laid up in some cool place, waiting for evening, and Hogan's stomach wasn't going to let him wait that long to eat.

Jakey was looking at a restaurant he could see from where they were sitting in the shade by the bayou and thinking of something else entirely. He was starving, and restaurants had food. There were ways to get the food, even without money, if you put your mind to it, and as hard as Hogan was thinking about fishing, he was putting his mind to it.

"We're not stealing anything else," Hogan said again, seeing what Jakey was looking at and knowing what he was thinking.

"How would you like a big, juicy hamburger, with pickles and onions, and a big malted milk, and french fries?" Jakey asked him, still looking at the restaurant and thinking. It wasn't really a restaurant at all, but a junky kind of highway hangout with a big gravel parking lot outside and probably a bunch of pinball machines inside. Places like that made the best hamburgers in the world.

"If you say anything else about hamburgers," Hogan told him, "I'm gonna kill you. I'm going to do it with my bare hands or die trying." He leaned back against the bank and closed his eyes. "If I die, I won't care either."

"I'm going over there and use their bathroom," Jakey decided, and Hogan was suspicious. "If you don't trust me, you can come, too." Jakey laughed, acting like he didn't care one way or the other.

Hogan didn't trust him a bit, but he was too tired to move and waited while Jakey went.

Twenty minutes later Jakey was back with hamburgers, french fries, and malted milks.

Jakey had made a deal with the owner—work in exchange for food—so they ate. It was delicious and saved their lives, and when they were done, Jakey gave Hogan his choice of jobs: pick up the parking lot of the Wildcat Drive-in and Grill, which made delicious hamburgers and had a big sign on a pole with a picture of something that looked like a purple tiger eating a gigantic hamburger, or sweep and mop the floor inside, a job that was messier but cooler.

27: Come and See
Church, Louisiana, 1330

A more miserable bunch of marines never existed, at least not in peacetime, and Sims, the oldest man in the squad, was probably the most miserable. You don't march two miles, double time for two, march, and double time again without its taking its toll on your body.

They had been able to get an extra ten miles out of the night, but they still had another fifteen or sixteen miles to go, and they couldn't take a chance on moving in the daylight.

They had stopped in a thin line of trees between two cotton fields a few hundred yards below a place called Come and See Church, in plenty of cover, considering there weren't any houses or roads around, and they could see someone coming long before anyone could see them. They'd left the pipeline above the town of Crowville and followed an abandoned railroad line east of the Tensas River. They'd found a low-water bridge for the crossing. The water was over the bridge, but only by a foot or so, so they'd taken off their boots and socks for the second time that night, this time to keep them dry. From there they'd followed a dirt road east two miles and crossed Highway 65 early in the morning. Sims, tired as he was, couldn't sleep past noon and so didn't try to. He lay trying to think of what the boys were likely to do if they were headed toward the bridge.

If the boys came to the bridge by way of the highway or railroad tracks, they would have to go a long way, maybe about a half a mile, up the bridge approach. They would be in sight of all the traffic on the bridge, and the chances were good that they'd get stopped before they got on the superstructure. It was a two-lane bridge with no sidewalk for pedestrians, so there were only two ways they could get across without getting stopped. They could wait till it got dark, leave their bicycles, and take the tracks, getting up and moving when there was no traffic, say, late at night when there weren't many cars, and lying down behind the guardrail when a car came by. That was the most dangerous thing they could do, though, because the gaps between the crossties were sometimes a foot wide, and there wasn't anything under them but a long drop to the river.

The second possibility they had, which wasn't likely, was the inspector's catwalk underneath. Sims and the squad had studied that bridge from every angle and planned to cross on the catwalk themselves. To get to it, the boys had first to discover the access ladder that ran up the side of the first pylon. That meant they would have to find the way under the bridge to the edge of the river, and it meant having the guts to climb a hand-over-hand steel ladder eighty feet straight up. If they got on the catwalk, they wouldn't have any trouble getting across; there was a ladder up to the road surface on the Vicksburg side; they wouldn't have to climb back down.

Moving carefully to keep from waking anybody, he crawled over to Turkey Jones and shook him awake. Turkey's eyes came open reluctantly, and he sat up. "Let's go over the map for tonight," Sims said. "I'm going to put you in charge." Jones looked at him, puzzled, and Sims explained, "I'm leaving in a few minutes."

There was only one real problem in the route to the bridge, and that was the lack of cover. This was cotton country, and every field was open area. If Sims walked the line of trees that surrounded each field, he would be tripling his distance, and that was something he couldn't afford to do. The best thing he could think to do was avoid people any way he could and, if they saw him, wave at them and keep going. If anybody stopped him and had questions, he would just have to have an answer ready, say he was looking for an Army survey unit that was working around there. If he could average two miles an hour, he'd be there before dark.

He would leave his backpack, eat something before he left, and wait for them under the bridge by the ladder.

Jones nodded and went back to sleep.

PART THREE

The Bridge

28: Old Wars, New Wars

It's easy to look at a map and, where the map shows a line across a river, imagine a bridge. If a person were in an airplane or a balloon high enough to see from Texas all the way across Louisiana to the Mississippi River, the area covered on the boys' highway map, the bridge at Vicksburg would look as thin as a cat's whisker. But come up on it from underneath, from river level and stand looking up. On that bridge the cars pass so high overhead that you can't hear them, and most times you can't even hear the trucks. Stand looking at the length of it. It would be a long bridge if it spanned only that part of the river from the bank to the second pylon; then count the pylons and see how from the Louisiana banks to the Mississippi banks there are seven pylons. When you stand looking up at such a bridge, it's a lot more than a line on a map. It's so real and over-poweringly massive it makes you tend to lose your balance.

Jakey and Hogan had to get off their bikes and push them. The road below the bridge was good enough to ride on, but nobody in his right mind would ride a bike close to something like that. If the bridge wasn't enough to make them nervous, the river was. Jakey was so busy looking out for possible dangers he stepped into his pedal, skinned his shin, and tumped his bike over anyway. Hogan didn't kid him about it because he'd almost done the same thing twice.

It was hard to talk and harder to hear. The river didn't seem to be making any noise, even where it first rammed, then rushed around the concrete pylons that divided its channel. It didn't seem to be the wind that made the noise either, but when Jakey talked, he had to talk extra-loud, and when Hogan answered him, his voice sounded like it was coming from a long way away.

"Let's camp," Jakey shouted. He pointed to a thicket back from the bank about a hundred yards. Hogan nodded, and they started pushing their bikes through the loose sandy dirt toward it.

They hid their bikes and pitched their tent there in the thicket, thick as any in the swamps but dry and sandy. They had trouble making the tent pegs stick in the sand and had to cut longer ones. Finally they were set up, and Jakey stretched out on his sleeping bag on the side of a hill and started looking at the bridge through the binoculars.

Back from the edge of the river and with trees behind them it was easier to talk.

"Well," Hogan said, "we're here." He sat down beside his cousin, tired and hungry again. Nothing would please him more than for Jakey to admit that he, too, was tired and say, "Let's go home."

But of course, Jakey wasn't going to. Now he was looking at the city of Vicksburg through the glasses, what he could see of it. Jakey didn't know it, but the place he'd picked to camp was less than a thousand yards from an old excavation that cut halfway across Delta Point. During the siege of Vicksburg General Grant had tried to dig a canal across that jut of land so Union gunboats could pass out of range of the rebel guns on the Vicksburg bluff. Many a Union soldier had stood or lain where the boys were now, looking at that city, at the bell tower of the old courthouse, thinking of what it would be like to be there, dressed in clean clothes, sitting down to a good dinner, and away from the miserable muck of their digging.

"You want to look?" Jakey said, and handed his cousin the glasses. "We're here, but that's where we want to go."

He got up and walked back down to the bridge, this time not letting it impress or scare hm so much. He threw some rocks as far out into the river as he could, to test his arm and his power because there was nothing to throw at and nothing to hit. He could barely see a splash where the rocks hit, the river was moving so fast. The river was powerful, he was ready to admit that. Then he turned away to find his best rock and noticed the huge pylon that was built farther up the bank to take the high water when it came. There was a ladder, a kind of fire escape, running right up the side of it to an iron grating catwalk under the bridge, and he could see it was the way across.

Back near the camp Hogan sat studying the building tops of Vicksburg. There was a quiet, an incredible stillness around him, as if Jakey had gone and would never be back. He shook that feeling out of his mind and started watching a boat pushing barges up the river, watching the wake of the propellers, watching it inch its way along till it was under the bridge and heading north into the open river.

A green-winged beetle started buzzing above his head, and the beetle was the loudest thing in the world. Something told him to look up, and when he did, he saw Jakey, standing on the catwalk under the bridge, with one hand cupped around his mouth calling to him, his other hand and arm waving.

29: The Bridge

In all his life Sims had never lost his head or panicked, not even in Korea, when it looked like he wouldn't make it through the night alive, and not now. In Korea he had let his body work mechanically and his mind concentrate on problems as they came up. His body now had the task of walking, and long after he had stopped feeling his legs, they continued to walk. His mind concentrated on finding the direction he wanted and the best way to get there.

East, always east, always toward the river. When there was something to go around, he went around toward the north, always listening for the sound of the highway.

Ever since Winnsboro they had been traveling through cotton fields—field after field after field, all identical except perhaps in the direction of the rows. What looked like east could actually be moving him toward the south, and south would put him too far below the bridge. He had to hear the sound of traffic soon, he reasoned; he had to.

As it turned out, he saw the highway before he heard it. The late afternoon sun flashed on the side of something moving, a windshield perhaps. He held his ground for a few moments to see if there would be others. If it really were the highway, there would be other cars or trucks with windshields in the same lane to flash. Then it happened: a flash, then another, and several more. A line of cars, the highway; he knew exactly where he was.

At the end of the field he was in there was the ever-present border of briars and thorns to slow him down; farmers used the briars like fences to say "Keep out," and if he were a farmer, the way the world was, he'd probably do the same thing. If anybody ever made the world over, though, he wished they'd make it without briars, or fences, or borders, or even countries. That would cut out half the problems and just about all the wars.

He crawled through, expecting to find the inevitable dirt road on the other side, and there was a road. But this time it was blacktopped, and on the other side of it, instead of another row of briars and another field, there were young trees, cottonwoods and sweet gums, and beyond the trees he could see the earthen revetment wall. He still had a hundred yards of wild weeds and stickers to get through; but he could hear the river now, and he could smell it. The slope of the wall was covered with kudzu to keep it from eroding, and the thick vines made climbing hard. Once he was on top, though, the hard part was over; he could see the river and the bridge.

Below the revetment wall was a dirt road that ran north to the bridge and then west alongside it, back up to the highway. In the trees where the road first turned west was where Sims and the squad had hidden their last cache of supplies—everything they'd need to cross the bridge and clean uniforms for the flag-raising ceremony and parade.

His first concern wasn't with the supplies, though, but with the boys. He'd taken all the chances he could take short of stealing a car or hitchhiking to get to the bridge before they did, and from the south side of the bridge, he had every reason to believe that he'd made it. When he saw their bicycle tracks in the loose dirt and their sleeping bags laid out on the side of the hill, he was afraid that he was too late. Then he looked up and saw them. The crazy one, the one called Jakey, was stretched out on his stomach on the catwalk, and the one he thought had good sense was on the ladder, seventy feet off the ground. Jakey wasn't just on his stomach but was leaning over the rail, trying to reach down and help the other one up.

Names were suddenly important. If the one on the ladder let go and made a grab, he was dead. If the one on the catwalk on top caught his arm, they both were dead.

"Hold onto that ladder," he shouted, not a screaming shout, because they might not hear that, but a drill command. And then he remembered the names. "Hogan. Hold onto that ladder." He pointed up at the other one. "Jakey, get back and sit down."

Jakey sat down, and Hogan held on.

"Now you on the ladder, Hogan," he barked. "Have you ever fallen from a ladder before? Say 'yes, sir,' or 'no, sir'; I can hear you fine."

"No, sir," he heard the boy call down. It was faint, but he could hear it.

"Well, you're not going to fall off now," he called back, with every bit of authority he could get out of his lungs. "Look up and concentrate on getting to the top . . . concentrate. You are in command. You don't have to say 'Yes, sir.' You are in command."

It was all working, but the boy was still frozen to the ladder. He was afraid to take a hand or foot off to make a move in either direction.

"You will go *up*," he shouted. "When you go up, you will not fall. You have never fallen from a ladder before, and you will not fall now."

Sims was about to say something else when Hogan reached up with his right hand and grabbed the rung above; his right foot followed the hand up, not quite at the same time but not more than a heartbeat behind. Then his left hand and foot moved, almost in slow motion, and he was a rung closer to the top. It was done in jerks, but it was done, and another reach and step kept it going. Sims was watching carefully, and watching was worse than being up on the ladder himself. He didn't trust himself to say anything else, not even "Keep going." It all seemed to be happening in a dream.

Then suddenly it was over. Both boys were safely on the catwalk, and it was better than what might have happened had both of them tried to climb down; but it created another kind of problem.

"Can you hear me?" he yelled up, and an arm waving from the catwalk told him that they could. "Okay," he told them, "sit down and don't move, and wait for me to come up."

He watched, and they both sat down.

30: The Catwalk

For a long time on this trip, since Sikes, when Jakey had stolen the beer, Hogan had realized something about his cousin from Memphis: Jakey Darby was different from other people. Most people are predictable; most of the time you've got a pretty good idea what they're going to do, but not with Jakey. Most of the time, Hogan suspected, Jakey didn't know himself what he was going to do or couldn't tell you what he'd done when he'd done it. That could be good or bad; but the good didn't do much for you, and the bad could get you killed.

"If we ever get out of this," Hogan told him, more

disgusted with himself than with his cousin, "I don't want you ever to talk to me again. I don't even want you looking in my direction."

"Wasn't climbing that ladder something?" Jakey said, grinning innocently like a cartoon cat. "I was so scared I almost peed in my jeans. What did you do, look down?"

Hogan didn't want to talk about it. "Just tell me what we're doing up here. For what did I almost die?"

"To get to see this," Jakey said, sweeping his arm out in front of them to mean the view. "This is like being on top of a mountain or something. You're getting to see something that few people ever get to see."

"Yeah, and what's that?" Cars, trucks, and buses were passing on the roadway not fifteen feet above their heads.

The catwalk was about two feet wide and with guardrails on both sides that came up to the boys' waists. Between the rails there wasn't anything but space, so if you lost your balance or tripped over something, there was still the chance that you could fall through, though you'd have to be pretty inept to have that happen. The whole catwalk, from where they were to as far as they could see, hung on pieces of angle iron that were welded to the side of the steel girders. There wasn't anything under the crosshatch grating of the walkway but 110 feet of air. The trouble with it all—the part Hogan didn't like—was the bright orange color. The steel under their feet and the

angle iron holding everything up were covered with
rust. Hogan wiped at the rust with his hand, and his
hand turned orange. "If they could see this down here,
they'd think twice about being up there."

Just because something was rusty didn't mean that
it was dangerous; that's why they had bridge inspec-
tors and catwalks in the first place, so people who
knew what they were doing could look at the bridge
and make sure it was still safe. Jakey started to explain that to Hogan, but something else that was
more interesting was happening. Sims had collected
his equipment and was about to start on the ladder.

31: The Bridge, 1930

With the boys sitting on their bottoms
and safe on the catwalk above, Sims started working
on the ground, trying to beat the oncoming darkness.
Later on, when all this was over, he might try to
think about how close the boys had come to getting
killed, either one or both of them, and get the shakes;
right now there just wasn't time. He needed twenty
minutes of daylight to get them across the river, and
the sun was going to start setting in five.

The first thing he had to do was get the kids' sleep-

ing bags and bikes back out of the way, which he did;
he was surprised to see the rifle and wondered how
they'd got it; then, so nobody could see anything from
the road above, he swept away the bike tracks with a
branch.

There were two coils of rope, each coil sixty feet, in
the supply cache, and he got those out. If something
happened and they got caught in the dark up there, it
wouldn't hurt to be on a rope together. He was about
to start up when he had another thought: The boys
might be hungry, so he broke open three of the daily
ration packages and took out the strips of dried beef.
If somebody was hungry, he might be weak; if he was
weak, he might be dizzy.

The sun began to set as he climbed the ladder. The
two boys on top watched him come while he, looking
up, concentrated on their faces. When he got closer,
they moved away and gave him room to get on the
catwalk. The look on his face was one of those looks
that say it all: disgust, disappointment, and down-
right unhappiness. All Hogan could say in their defense was "From the ground it didn't look so high."

There wasn't enough time to give them a lecture,
so Sims didn't try. Instead, he took a coil of rope from
around his neck and undid it. He handed one end to
Hogan and showed him how to fashion it into a harness. Without having to stand up, Hogan was able to
loop it under his arms and between his legs; then

Sims gave the other end to Jakey and had him do the same thing.

"Okay," he said, "we're a long way up; but the grating isn't going to break, and we're not going to fall out the sides." He looked at Hogan and tried to decide whether or not he might again freeze. The key was what he could get the other one to do, he decided, and turned to Jakey. "You're not afraid of where you are, are you?" Jakey shook his head no. "Then I want you to stand up and walk about twenty paces, stop, and sit down."

Jakey thought it was a strange request but got up and did it. Sims found the middle of the rope, made his own harness, and tied himself in; then he turned to Hogan and gave him the plan. "We're going to cross. Jakey's going to go first, I'll be in the middle, and you'll bring up the rear. We're all tied together, so nothing can happen. We'll be twenty yards apart, so even if a whole section of grating falls through, which it won't, there'll be two of us safe to pull the third person up." He motioned for Jakey to stand up, and they moved till the rope was stretched taut to Hogan; then Hogan rose, and they started across. In fifteen minutes, Sims hoped, the boys' long adventure would be over.

The walking, once they learned to trust the cat-walk, wasn't difficult and, for Jakey, was almost enjoyable. At first Hogan couldn't help watching his feet as he walked, and looking down at his feet meant looking through the open holes in the grating to the river below. The river wasn't brown anymore, but almost a solid black in the approaching darkness. When they got halfway across, it got easier for Hogan to look up, as if he could relax more by concentrating on where he was going, though "relax" was not the right word. The sunset behind them was in the bright red final stages, and the city of Vicksburg in that strange light looked seriously wrong, as though somebody had taken a color picture of it and printed the negative; everything was dark green, black, or red.

Sims, ahead of him, was looking at the same thing and thinking of something completely different. He was amused at how obvious it was that the city had been founded by somebody with a military mind. There weren't many places with such military importance easier to defend: Gibraltar, for sure, because it controlled the Mediterranean; West Point, maybe, because it controlled the Hudson. There were places more important, like Panama, but they weren't natural fortresses, and there were better natural fortresses, like some of the robbers' roosts out West, but they weren't very strategically important. Vicksburg had been settled by a military mind, probably one of the finest.

Jakey Darby, leading the way, was wondering what he could do to keep the game from ending. Vicksburg wasn't something to be happy about, not when it meant everything's being over and his going back to Nothingsville Farm, Nowheresville, Louisiana. He knew what he could count on back there, and that was cows in the morning and his toes at night.

They had been listening to the sound of sirens for some time now, off and on since they'd started across the river, but sirens could mean anything; it was hard sometimes *not* to hear them. By the time they were within a hundred yards of the bank it had become highly probable that the sirens had something to do with them. It was much darker now, and they could see the flashing red lights of police cars reflecting off the bridge's upper struts.

Jakey was just about to get his wish.

32: Pinning It All Down

At seven-thirty that evening, when the kids and Sims were on the bridge and almost in Mississippi, Gilbert and the other McGhees, Pigiron and Benny, and an FBI agent named Portwood were on the old church bus headed in that direction. They were past Tallulah and no more than fifteen minutes from the bridge with one Louisiana Highway Patrol car in front and another one in back. It was an official police motorcade, in contact with each other and with the Mississippi Highway Patrol and FBI agents on the bridge ahead by means of radio.

The FBI got involved with it all when the Caldwell Parish sheriff in Columbia called them, but that's taking things out of order. First, the McGhees left the pharmacy in Sikes, heading toward Columbia. When they got there, they were met by the sheriff and stopped at a Quik Mart, where they talked to Dr. Johnson and the owner of the store, who identified Hogan's picture. The doctor didn't press charges on the forgery, but he made Gilbert McGhee promise to impress on his kids the serious nature of forging a medical doctor's name. In some states it was a prison offense. The sheriff asked Pigiron a lot of questions when he found out about the nine or ten soldiers, but the most important was "Could they have been marines?" and things began to make a little more sense. The name Jakey Darby was one the store owner remembered from somewhere, and then he remembered where. In that morning's paper was a picture of a Jakey Darby, the same, winning a pie-eating contest in Mangham. The sheriff of Caldwell Parish in Columbia called the sheriff of Richland Parish in Mangham and the FBI in Monroe. That was how the FBI got involved.

The sheriff in Mangham looked, dressed, and acted like Roy Rogers, and all the girls fell in love with him. He had a photographer following him around, somebody from the local newspaper, and they took a million pictures, putting on a show for the girls and the federal officers. The sheriff's office had a contract with a business in town that supplied box lunches for big operations, and if this wasn't a big operation, nothing was. By the time they had all eaten and answered the FBI's questions and finally got around to looking at some maps and figured out that the kids and missing marines were all heading to Vicksburg, it was six-thirty. The FBI agent named Portwood radioed ahead and got authorization for a roadblock check at the tollhouse on the Mississippi side. The photographer called ahead to some of his newspaper chums in Vicksburg and tipped them off that the famous missing marines were on their way and would cross the bridge that night.

It was all very complicated and was going to get even more complicated. The Mississippi Highway Patrol had even sent for a helicopter.

33: Vicksburg

Nothing was ever easy, Sims was thinking. Just when you get to thinking you have it made, that's when you'd better watch out the most because something's sure enough about to go wrong.

The way off the catwalk should have been easy compared to the way on: It was only a ten-foot climb on a short ladder to the road surface above and from there only a fifty-foot run to the bank. With it dark he should have been able to slip the kids up the ladder and off the bridge easy; it was just a matter of timing.

But of course, it wasn't. The flashing lights alone could have told them that. To find out how bad it was, Sims climbed up and poked his head between the guardrails; it didn't take but a second to see what was going on; in that second he saw at least four uniformed poliemen and what looked like two more in plain clothes. There was a crowd of people standing around, watching everything, floodlights, a regular roadblock.

Sims came back down and shook his head. "They're stopping and searching everything," he told them. "The traffic's backed up all the way to here."

Jakey didn't hesitate for a minute; he recognized the problem and volunteered, "What do you want us to do?"

"First of all, eat something," Sims said, and handed them the dried beef.

That wasn't hard, considering how little they'd eaten that day.

"There's another way off the bridge," he said, and told them his idea. First of all, they'd use the ropes. The two of them each would be in harness so they couldn't fall no matter what happened. He would walk the other ends over to the bank and tie them off to the beams.

"Then what?" Hogan asked.

"Well," Sims said, "you might not want to do this, and I'm not even sure you should try." What he had in mind was their jumping off the end of the catwalk and swinging over into the side of the bluff. That would be swinging from a height of fifty feet into the side of a bank they couldn't see. Then it would mean pulling themselves or his pulling them up to the top of the bank.

Even Jakey thought that was a bad idea. "Why don't we all just walk the beams?" he suggested. If he fell, he'd rather hit the bank from thirty feet or even closer. "All you have to do is hold the rope over the beam and keep taking up the slack," he suggested. "That way we don't break our legs."

There was a chance that way that they might hit their heads on the beam when they fell, Sims told them.

"There's also a better chance that we won't fall," Jakey said back.

"When you're old enough to join something and

want to join the Marines," Sims said, "look me up. I want you guys in my outfit."

Hogan didn't know if Sims was calling him brave or dumb.

Structural beams like the ones they were going to try to walk were called *I* beams because when you looked at them from the ends, they looked like the capital letter *I*. The top part of the *I* was barely wider than their shoes, so it was going to be quite a balancing act. They would have some help, though, because it wasn't a single beam running to the bank but two, one they'd walk on and one above their heads they could hold onto. The real problems were the cross braces; some they'd have to duck, some they'd have to step over, and some they'd have to swing out around.

Sims didn't think there was much chance that they could get hurt, some bumps and bruises maybe, but that was about all. He got them tied into their harnesses and tied the ropes to the catwalk. If he fell, he didn't want them pulled off the catwalk. Then, with the other end of the rope Jakey was tied to, he made his own harness. The other end of Hogan's rope he tied to his belt.

Then he climbed over the handrail and got on the beam. "Just concentrate on getting to the bank. Watch what you're doing, and stay on the outside of that crosspiece."

They watched Sims cross to the bank, and it looked easy; but then Sims made it look easy because he was good at that kind of thing. On the bank he looped the ropes around the beam and tied them off. Now it was up to the boys. "Why don't you go first?" Jakey suggested. "I went first last time."

Somehow or other, Jakey could make even the dumbest of ideas seem reasonable. Indeed, he had gone first the last time; that was how they had got into this mess in the first place.

Hogan did it, though. He climbed over the rail and started to the bank, working slowly, working carefully, ducking under the first piece, stepping over the next. Then he was in the middle and had to move his hands from the piece above to the one he was stepping around, and he did it with more confidence. Ten more feet, and he wasn't over river anymore but over good Mississippi earth; five more feet after that, and he could jump down.

It was Hogan Sims had been worried about, and it was Jakey who fell. He got halfway, but when he shifted his hands, he tried to do it too quickly; what he actually did was make an awkward grab, and the next thing, before he even knew what was happening, he was swinging in space. Sims held the rope and watched him swing into the bank, well above it instead of into the side of it, and then back out again over the river. Sims judged the distance between the rope and the bank, and just as Jakey reached the end of his backswing out, he slackened the rope about five feet, and Jakey thought he was going to die. He was just about to start yelling when, instead of falling, he started back to the bank, and this time he landed on the run.

They had arrived in Mississippi, and there was only one more thing they had to do. After they had calmed down enough to pay attention, Sims explained it to them.

In the movies it would have been called a diversionary tactic.

34: Fault Lines

Somewhere between Tallulah and the bridge Grandma McGhee fell asleep. She was sitting behind Gilbert, who was driving the bus, listening to the sirens and watching the sunset, when all of a sudden she couldn't keep her eyes open. She'd fallen asleep for a short nap at this time of day for so many years habit took over, and she leaned her head against the window and started snoring.

Once they climbed the ramp and were on the

bridge, the patrolmen driving the escort cars turned the sirens off. They couldn't pass anybody on the two-lane roadway, and there wasn't anywhere for a car in their way to pull off. About halfway across, they had to slow to a crawl behind the long line of cars and trucks that were backed up by the roadblock, and Gilbert found himself again trying to make some sense out of the day's events.

First of all, there wasn't any doubt now that it was the nine marines who had disappeared from Houston that they were looking for. Pigiron's pinpointing the places where the marines had camped let the FBI people find the garbage dumps and take fingerprints. It was them all right.

Secondly, there was no doubt that they were on their way to Vicksburg. They had orders, the marine investigators had discovered, ordering them to report for reveille and parade duties on July the Fourth, which was tomorrow. If they hadn't done anything to entice the two boys to follow them, and if they hadn't done anything to make the boys steal for them, there was some doubt that the marines could even be charged with a crime. The only thing anybody could think of was reckless endangerment, but for that charge to stick, they had to cause somebody to get either killed or hurt. If they didn't get caught on the bridge, which was a misdemeanor, they'd be home safe.

His natural instinct as a father was to blame it all on Jakey. If Jakey hadn't come for his visit, none of this would've happened. Hogan might have accidentally discovered the marines when they came through, but he wouldn't have followed them, not by himself. He'd have turned them in to the sheriff and put a stop to it. Blaming Jakey was too easy, though, because Hogan was in it all the way and was maybe more to blame; he ought to have had better sense. Shirley had sent her boy down here to get their help in keeping him out of trouble, and here was Hogan getting in it with him.

So whose fault was it really? In a way it was his own fault for not watching them more closely. He had, after all, let them go for a long time before he went after them, and if one of them got hurt, he'd never forgive himself.

But he knew where the blame should really go: It should go to the challenge, to their being boys, boys who are thirteen years old and want to grow up too fast, who are not afraid of anything and think nothing can kill them, ever. It wasn't hard to remember what he himself had been like at thirteen; it had been during the Depression, and he and a boy named John Robert Pesky, whom Grandma McGhee still wrinkled her nose at and called "that Pesky boy," had run away to New Orleans to ship out on a freighter. They hadn't made it much past Cheneyville before they were broke, hungry, and wet from the rain. He was never so happy to get caught in his whole life. He would blame it on something like the challenge.

They were stuck on the bridge for about fifteen minutes before somebody at the roadblock figured out what to do. "Church bus motorcade, this is Mississippi command," the radio cracked. "Look, we've got to get you off that bridge, so we're stopping traffic over here. We're sending a patrol car over with the light going, so when it gets by you, you'll know it's safe to pull out and pass." That was simple enough, and they could see the patrol car coming. It zoomed on by, and the patrol car leading the motorcade hit its siren again. Gilbert swung the church bus out and gave it some gas, and that's when Grandma McGhee woke up. She saw what that old bus was trying to pass, then she looked down and saw how high they were over the river and how thin the guardrail was between the bus and the river and let out a crazy war whoop. The girls had to grab her before she got to the door, or she'd have tried to jump from the bus to safety.

It would've been tragic if Grandma McGhee had been the one to suffer, but she was stronger than anyone gave her credit for being.

In five minutes they were in Mississippi and talking to another FBI man, this time the agent who was in charge of the whole operation.

"Is that the dog that started out following them?" he wanted to know, and Pigiron said yes. "You think he might still have the scent?" he asked, and there wasn't any doubt in Pigiron's mind.

They took the dog down to the bridge and held traffic again while he sniffed the roadway. They could tell that he was on to something but was still confused about where it was coming from. They took him over to the railroad part of the bridge and had him try it there, and that wasn't it. Then Pigiron took him under the bridge, and there it was, the place where the boys had climbed from the beams, the ropes they'd used, and the fresh scent of where they had gone. Benny got so excited by hitting a trail so fresh after so long a track all he could do was send up a howl.

"They've crossed over," Pigiron said, showing the direction around the side of the tollhouse hill where the railroad tracks came off the bridge and cut through the side of the grade.

Gilbert looked at the beams they'd walked to get to the bank and shivered. Even when he was thirteen, he'd never tried anything like that.

35: Mission Complete

The diversionary tactic that Sims asked them for was right up Jakey's alley. At last they were in a city, a real city, and though it wasn't as big as Memphis, it was big enough to hide in for an hour or so, then get caught someplace in town, someplace away from the bridge. He showed them how they could follow the train tracks around the side of the hill below and out of sight of the roadblock, through the tunnel under the highway and out into the park. The park was probably the easiest place for them to hide in; but Jakey was tired of hiding, and Sims had given them five dollars to use in case they needed it.

"Where do you get these crazy ideas?" Hogan was complaining. The tracks swung back toward the river and the railroad yards north of the bridge. When it passed under the highway again, Jakey had decided they should get up on top and rejoin civilization. It was a thirty-foot bank they had to climb, covered with weeds and cinders, and the reason Hogan was complaining was that he was slipping so often and with such regularity that he had to go up three feet to get one. "What part of your warped personality thinks these things up?"

Jakey, for some reason, was going up the hill with no trouble, as though being in a city again had given him supernatural powers. He could see streetlights;

he could hear horns blowing and smell people. "Can't you just feel it?" he said, throwing his head up in the air like a coyote sniffing the wind and beating on his chest like Tarzan. He hadn't realized how out of place he'd been till he got up on top and found himself on a real street with a real sidewalk.

"Now what, Sherlock?" Hogan said, looking around at where they were.

The answer to the question of what to do next turned out to be the easiest answer in their whole trip. They started walking north toward downtown Vicksburg, and there on the first corner, on a telephone pole, was a green and white sign that said "Bus Stop." They took the bus downtown, got off and looked around for a while, and got something to eat at a café called the Glass Kitchen, which Hogan thought was strange. The wall to the kitchen was about half glass, so you watched the cooks cooking and washing dishes and mopping the floor. Most places Hogan had been, they wanted to hide the kitchen, not show it off. He had a bacon, lettuce, and tomato sandwich and watched them cook it and fix it; Jakey had two hamburgers, a glass of milk, and for the first time in his life a cup of coffee. They sat at the counter instead of a booth, and the waitress watched Jakey to see what he did with the cream and sugar she'd pushed at him. He didn't really know what he was supposed to do and decided he liked his coffee black.

The coffee was much too hot to drink, and he was trying a trick that he'd seen men do, melting a piece of ice in a spoon to catch the water, hoping to cool it off. Hogan was watching the operation, thinking how silly it was to get something hot, like coffee, and then want to cool it off with ice. Outside on the sidewalk a dog came walking, his nose down searching. Behind him walked a tall, wild-looking man, and behind them both in the street came police cars and a purple and gold bus. As oddly as the kids' adventure had begun, except for the loose ends, it suddenly ended.

EPILOGUE

36: The Loose Ends

During the Civil War Vicksburg was so important to the Union cause that Lincoln sent his best generals, Grant and Sherman, to take the city. They made seven major assaults on the Confederate fortress, from the river, against the high ground by way of Steele's Bayou and another attack up the Yazoo River, and from the west. All told, the campaign lasted from November 1862 till the middle of May 1863 with the Union forces of more than 70,000 men being fought to a standstill by a Confederate force of only 20,000. In May Grant decided to lay siege and starve the people out, but even that was not easy. The city defenders rationed their food; then, when it was gone, they ate their mules and horses;

and finally, they ate the huge, black-furred water rats. On the verge of starvation, General Pemberton, the Confederate general, surrendered on the Fourth of July, and Grant was so respectful and proud of the fight the outnumbered rebels had made, he let the officers keep their sidearms.

After almost a hundred years there were still quite a few Vicksburgers who refused to celebrate the Fourth of July with any kind of patriotic activity and a few diehards, it was rumored, who mourned the day by symbolically eating rats.

But there were more people who did celebrate and who braved the day's heat at the national cemetery to see the famous missing marines or lined the streets around the courthouse to see the parade. In all fairness, the marines' big show was the flag raising at the cemetery, with all the newspaper and television reporters there to see them come marching out of the woods.

The Vicksburgers who turned out for the parade did so because they wanted to see the two kids who'd followed the marines across the state of Louisiana and across the river under the bridge. It had been announced on television and on the radio that the boys would be in the parade, and indeed, they were.

But first things first. A lot of things happened after they'd got caught. First they were questioned by the FBI agent who wanted to know where the marines were, and Jakey, who was the more skilled at lying, told about how they had watched the squad cross the bridge on the catwalk and followed them and how when they got to the Mississippi side, the squad's ropes had been there to show them how to get off without being seen. The marines, Jakey figured, were hiding somewhere in the park.

That story got the FBI to stop the roadblock, forget about the bridge, and concentrate their efforts in the park.

After that, still sitting in the Glass Kitchen restaurant, they were interviewed by a Colonel Linco, who wanted to know if the marines had forced them to do anything: to follow them, to steal, or to get on the bridge. Hogan took over then because he wouldn't have to lie and told the colonel about how he and Jakey had done everything on their own. The last they saw of the colonel, he was in a phone booth calling somebody in Washington and yelling, "I don't care what time it is, get him and put him on the phone."

After that all they had to do was face the music again from Hogan's father, and they wouldn't have to do that till they got back home.

Sims, on the other side of the river again while all this was going on, waited for the rest of the squad to get there and, while he waited, managed to get some sleep. By the time the others got there the bridge was long deserted. Traffic was down to a car or two an hour, and crossing was easy. Once in Mississippi, they rappelled the bluff and moved north along the bank till they were in the railroad yards, then farther north between long lines of sidetracked boxcars till they were north of the city, below Chickasaw Bluffs and Fort Hill and the cemetery. A spring came through there, and they bathed in it and changed into their clean uniforms. After that all they had to do was wait where they were and try to stay clean till morning.

They'd wanted to get some good publicity for the Marine Corps, and they got it. The newspeople and the crowd got there early and watched to see what was going to happen and were set up and waiting. Just before the ceremony was scheduled to begin, the squad climbed over the cemetery wall and formed ranks. Sims marched them proudly up to the marine lieutenant he was ordered to report to. He saluted, and the lieutenant returned the salute and transferred the folded triangle of flag to the sergeant. They saluted each other again, and Sims did a smart about-face and led the squad to the base of the flagpole where Turkey Jones stepped from ranks and held the rope steady while Sims attached the flag. For this ceremony, there was no band. There was just a solo bugler, a young boy in Navy summer whites with a single black stripe below the bugle symbol on his sleeve. The lieutenant gave the signal to begin, "Present Arms," and the boy, standing alone before the neat, white tombstones that stretched out of sight behind him, blew the call and the flag went up. It was done crisply, the way things were meant to be done; it brought goose bumps to the back of the necks of everybody there, and tears to the eyes of many.

The parade wasn't so serious. There were lots of bands and people marching, and at the end of it all, as if they had been following the whole thing, came the boys on their bicycles. The parade organizers had sent a truck over to get them and bring them for the show, and it turned out well. People got to see them and wave, and they got to wave back. It was the kind of victory parade that made people just plain feel good.

After the parade, Grandma McGhee, the girls, Pigiron, and Benny were all bone tired and needed to get back to the farm, and there wasn't any reason, other than vain glory-seeking, for them to stay. They loaded the bikes, Jakey's rifle, and the other equipment on the bus and went home.

In the week that followed, the boys got a letter from Sims to thank them for their help (and for keeping quiet about the bridge). In the letter he mentioned that he and the men in the squad were fine, in no trouble, and that there was talk of their being reassigned to embassy duty somewhere in the Far East. He, for one, hoped so.

Shirley, Jakey's mother, came to visit, to see what was going on and make some decisions about the future. If any decisions were made, though, she didn't tell Jakey or Hogan what they were.

In the week after that, things started getting back to

normal. For Jakey, normal meant boring, and he was busy at work thinking up some new project to get involved with. He and Hogan went fishing a lot and were probably pestering Pigiron too much.

Then, just when Jakey was so bored he was about to do something drastic, everything changed: The McGhees got a long-distance telephone call from Hollywood, California. Everybody was somewhere doing something, except Grandma McGhee, who was home alone and took the call. It was from a man who wanted to know if it was all right for him to come to Natchitoches and talk to the boys.

Grandma McGhee couldn't imagine why anybody would want to come that far just to talk, but she didn't see anything wrong with his doing it, if that's what he wanted to do, and told him to come ahead.

The man, of course, had more on his mind than just talk. He wanted to make a movie about the boys and the marines, and he had contracts in his pocket for everybody to sign.

So he could have a part in the movie, Jakey stayed in Louisiana the rest of the summer and enrolled in school in Natchitoches. He and Hogan both had big parts to start with, but as it turned out, neither one of them could act worth a hoot and their parts were trimmed down; the stunt men who dressed in their clothes had more time in front of the camera than the boys had. The "marines" had the biggest parts and the biggest stars playing them, and the story writers who kept changing the script kept making up stuff for "Sims" and the squad to do, stuff that never happened. It made the boys look kind of dumb in the long run, and soured Jakey on movies forever.

He and Hogan thought about it, after it was all over and the dust had settled. It was summer again, and hot, and they were in their upstairs bedroom trying to figure out what to do next. Jakey was lying on his bed with his legs hanging out the window, letting mosquitoes in. "Did you ever think about going to sea?" he asked, finally, and Hogan gave out one of his famous groans.